The Heavens
Weep
For Us

AND OTHER STORIES

To Pierrette –
Thank you for
your supportiveness.
Best wishes!

Thelma T. Reyna

3-9-10

Outskirts Press, Inc.
Denver, Colorado

Outskirts Press, Inc.
http://www.outskirtspress.com

ISBN: 978-1-4327-3071-0

Outskirts Press and the "OP" logo are trademarks belonging to Outskirts Press, Inc.

PRINTED IN THE UNITED STATES OF AMERICA

Praise for Thelma T. Reyna's
The Heavens Weep for Us and Other Stories

" ...I love and respect this work."

--Tiffany Ana Lopez, Ph.D.,
Author of *Growing Up Chicana/o*

"Beautiful short stories....brilliant writer...as good as Jhumpa Lahiri, Sandra Cisneros, J. California Cooper, or Philip Roth, for that matter."

--Robin D. G. Kelley, Ph.D.,
Author of *Race Rebels* and *Hammer and Hoe*

"In this engaging debut collection, Thelma Reyna introduces us to ordinary people whose lives are shaped by fatalism and irony. The characters are Latinos from diverse social stratas, but their stories resonate with universal truths. Reading her stories is like opening a gift, evoking both pleasure and surprise."

--Rose Guilbault,
Author of *Farmworker's Daughter*

"Thelma...beautiful story. You are quite talented."

--Daniel A. Olivas,
Author of *Latinos in Lotusland: An Anthology of Contemporary Southern California Literature*

"I was intrigued how you take mundane life...and you make the story marvelous. I thoroughly enjoyed this little nutmeg book; like life, it is full of sweets and spices—a surprising savory read."

--Mark Lamonica,
Author of *Whacking Buddha* and *Junkyard Dogs and William Shakespeare*

Dedication

To my radiant young treasures: my son, Victor Cass, and his daughter, Elizabeth; my daughter, Christine Reyna-Demes, her husband Chuck Demes, and their children, Charlie and Cassandra.

To my radiant "mellowed-like-fine-wine" treasure: my supportive, caring husband, Victor Reyna, who also happens to be the coolest "Papa" in the world. Just ask Lizzie, Charlie, and Cassie!

To the memory of my mother, Mary G. Ruth, from Kingsville, Texas, who always encouraged me to write. She awaited this book with quiet pride and recently slipped away to watch over us from a better place.

Introduction
By Robin D.G. Kelley, Ph.D.*

Thelma Reyna is a truly gifted individual. She possesses a kind of second sight, a rare ability to penetrate the masks and facades we mere mortals use to protect our most intimate thoughts, fears, and anxieties, and unveil the truth. And she has this uncanny ability to find language to express those feelings and experiences that just seem too big or too painful or too beautiful for words. She is no mere wordsmith; rather, she is a sensitive listener who understands humanity in all of its dimensions.

I recognized these qualities in Thelma long before I discovered her talent as a writer. Between 1978-1980, she was my English and Creative Writing teacher at Pasadena High School in Pasadena, California. It was a huge, inadequately funded school that served mostly low-income Black and Latino students. I was one of those students, an African-American son of a single mother who, like most kids in my cohort, was tracked for low-wage service work, prison, or, at best, a stint at Pasadena City College or Los Angeles Trade Tech. Thelma never accepted our presumed fate, because she could see capacity and possibility where others could not. She pulled from our narratives truths that had been suppressed for so long---a "thug's" romantic streak, a young hustler's love for mathematics or theater, a kid marked "remedial" capable of rendering her dismal neighborhood into a fantastic carnival. Thelma brought us back to life by helping us discover our inner resources and the force that animates us: Love. Although she never said it directly, she taught us that love was the path to self-recovery, since it enabled us to see and accept all the dimensions of who we were and who we could be. Her teaching was transformative.

Reading her beautiful collection of short stories three decades later, I recognize the same visionary, transformative qualities she brought to her teaching. The work is vivid, alive, soul-penetrating, and as powerful as anything by Jhumpa Lahiri, Sandra Cisneros, J. California Cooper, or Philip Roth, for that matter. Reyna has this amazing ability to float into a life-in-progress and reveal the social, physical, and emotional landscapes with exacting precision.

And the themes are universal—her stories are about the fleeting, transient nature of love and life. Relationships, even those with the strongest bonds, are always tenuous and vulnerable, and everything can change as a result of a chance encounter. There is no divine justice or plan, yet there is something divine and huge about how we find our unique paths to love, how we cope with loss, and how all of these travels help us find who we are. Nothing is inevitable, and, unlike the planets, there is nothing keeping human beings from drifting apart, drifting toward each other, being cruel or being kind.

I had this revelation reading stories like "Little Box" and "Comatose" and "White Van," which remind us that we really are vulnerable, sort of like living on top of a building without a railing, or walking a tightrope without a net. We make choices, yet our compass is embedded in our emotions more so than in our rational intellect.

I was struck by how "White Van" is entirely interior, an encounter that never actually takes place, yet it is paradoxically profound. I love how Diego in "Marry Me" becomes the vehicle for us to know Kika's story and to discover the fleeting yet powerful nature of love. On the other hand, stories like "Faithless" and "Saving Up" reveal that, while love is tenuous and often fleeting, memories are not. We don't forget, even if we wanted to. We carry them with us, and they can haunt us, or make us smile. I like the irony, too, of a comatose woman remembering.

Finally, "The Heavens Weep for Us" is pure poetry. As tragic as it is, in some ways it sums up some of the themes in Reyna's stories. I read it as a meditation on domestic violence, which sometimes, ironically, is the darkest side of love's tenuous nature. We are held together by so little, and yet emotionally it is all so big. There is no divine intervention here, and that is exactly the point. It is also a challenge to all of us to make different choices, and to cease being silent in the face of brutality.

I could go on. Thelma Reyna's stories are excellent, and I enjoyed reading every word. While they are often filled with pain, they speak to the human spirit—not as some larger-than-life powerful force (which is the common analogy), but as something vulnerable, precious, delicate, and yet persevering. The lesson is revelatory and yet eerily familiar, for if there was anything I took from Thelma Reyna's Creative Writing class thirty years ago, it is that we are vulnerable, precious, delicate, and persevering. These are the qualities that make us human.

#

* Dr. Kelley is the author of several books, among them *Race Rebels, Hammer and Hoe* and, most recently, *Freedom Dreams*. His biography of jazz pianist and composer Thelonious Monk will be published by Simon and Schuster in 2009. He has taught at the University of Michigan, Columbia University, New York University, and is currently a professor at the University of Southern California.

Author's Foreword

When one of my short stories, "Una Edad Muy Tierna, M'ija" ("A Very Tender Age, My Daughter") was included in Tiffany Ana Lopez' anthology, *Growing Up Chicana/o* in 1993, I stated the following in my author's blurb about influences on my writing:

> *Loss* was a reality that colored many of my perceptions about growing up, and it was an inevitable companion to *love*. ...It seems, unfortunately, that the events most filling my "writing mind" are painful ones.

Today, as I finished organizing my stories for this book, I realized that this theme still pervades my writings. My daughter, a university professor in Chicago and herself a published author, recently asked me why this is so. My son, also a published author, has likewise asked me over the years why my characters suffer as they do. I haven't been able to explain it adequately, for I'm not wholly sure of the reason. All I can say is the following:

Loss is memorable, as is pain. This is why a soldier recalling a battle forty years after the fact still weeps in the retelling, why a mother reliving a child's accident from decades ago still trembles, why a man recalling a long-ago lover can still feel the pangs of their parting. The pain of their losses might have blurred, and their days go on with a veneer of acceptance and of forgetting, for life always does go on. It must.

But beneath the veneer that the past is gone, dead and gone, is a transparent film of pain that doesn't ever wholly leave. And this pain is something that adds a deeper dimension to our existence in this world, something that sharpens the days of joy for us, that brightens for our eyes the bird singing with abandon in the trees with buds just sprouting.

The loss I describe in my writings is not necessarily the loss of life itself, but losses such as those that pepper our daily existence in ways large and small: the loss of faith, the loss of independence, the loss of opportunities, and so on. I believe that loss of any type diminishes to some extent the general well-being of the person bearing that loss; but imbedded in the emotions attending loss are opportunities for redemption, for insights, for evolution of our selves. I also believe that the counterweight to loss is love—the "greatest of these"—and that the two are inextricably entwined.

As I reflect upon the people in this collection of stories—Petra, Paula, Kika, Maggie, Faith, Manuel, Juana Macho, Pablo, etc.—I am reminded of how they responded to their distinct losses in ways that required them to dig deeply into their *selves*. My characters are a motley crew of Californians, Texans, and Chicagoans who run the gamut from struggling immigrant to wealthy American, educated and not, sophisticated and not, faithful and not. My Hispanic heritage may be apparent in names I choose for them and in settings I root them. But it's my hope that the characters you meet in this book resonate with you, that they come across to you as what they are: simply, human beings facing whatever befalls them with all the dignity and courage they can muster.

Here's to them…and you!

Thelma T. Reyna
Pasadena, California
May 2009

Table of Contents

* Published in the Spring 2009 issue of *Chicana/Latina Studies: The Journal of Mujeres Activas en Letras y Cambio Social (The Journal of Women Active in Letters and Social Change), Volume 8.* Edited by Drs. Karen Mary Davalos & Tiffany Ana Lopez.

"...I write what I see, what's told to me that I feel very deeply, or what happened to me that I can't forget, but also what happened to others I love, or what strangers have told me happened to them, or what I read happened to others. I take all of this and cut and paste it together to make a story, because in real life a story doesn't have shape, and it's the writer that gives it a beginning, a middle, and an end."

--Sandra Cisneros
Poet, Novelist, Short Story Writer
In www.sandracisneros.com

White Van

Why did she feel so compelled to make eye contact, to nod at him in recognition, to wave as she drove by, ...with the white van itself between the two of them?

White Van

She had lived in the neighborhood a little more than two weeks when she first noticed him. He lived across the street from her, or almost across the street: his house faced Hill Avenue and hers faced Brookstone Street. If she stood in her front yard to water her plants, she could see him in his if he happened to be outdoors.

But he seemed to go outside only in the mornings and the evenings. He was just an old man, a pot-bellied stump of a man, chalky-wispy hair emanating like frail spokes around his thick, round head, stubble on his face...or at least what she thought was stubble, from where she was each time she saw him: either driving past his house early in the morning on her way to work, or glimpsing him from eighty yards away in the afternoons as she puttered in her yard and he in his.

The first time she noticed him, he was standing in his

3

front yard, stock-still, feet planted shoulder-width, hands clasped behind his back. He looked like a soldier at parade rest, she'd thought as she gazed at him from her van at the corner stop sign: like an attentive soldier, except that the faded olive green tank top undershirt, the old-fashioned ribbed-knit type with huge armpit openings, was the farthest thing from military discipline. He stood in his yard just like that, an old soldier in the middle of his front yard, arms behind his back, his head craned skyward. She was at the stop sign waiting for the morning traffic to zip by, and something about how he stood there alone had caught her eye. Curious, she had stuck her neck out her van's window and looked at the sky in the direction he was staring.

Circling and swooping in slow motion was a soundless plane spewing cotton-puff letters that waved and melted almost as quickly as the plane birthed them, so that, after a while, only trembling round dots of clouds wafted in immense blueness. She was able to see the message, though, the message that had evidently captured the old man's attention: "Last Chance to Talk to God." As her white van crossed the intersection, she slowed past his house and could have sworn that he'd been smiling, as his face—and were those tears?—remained upturned. He never moved a muscle.

The next morning, as she drove past his brown clapboard house on the corner lot, she saw him stepping outside.

The Heavens Weep for Us

Again, he wore the undershirt, hair Einstein-inspired, a nappy, yippy little dog bouncing near his ankles. The man was empty-handed and gingerly picked his way down his four concrete steps on the front stoop. He stepped onto the grass, head down. He did not notice her as she zoomed by.

Her morning focus was generally absorbed by the radio news as she drove to work, and by the challenges she knew she'd face that day on the job. It was her job, after all, a fast-paced, demanding career, that had spurred her move to California. She'd left old friends and all her family halfway across the nation at the beginning of summer to seek her professional fortunes in Pasadena. This neighborhood, touted by her real estate agent as a place "where children can grow up safely" and "your neighbors will become your family," was her landing spot. Yes, the tall trees lining the streets on both sides, the mountains looming as far as she could see and turning lavender in the cool evenings gave her some measure of joy in living on this block, in this city. But this place was only her landing spot. She didn't deceive herself that any other roots would form.

There was something about the old man that interested her, however. His wardrobe never differed. His hair was subject to no comb's rule—resulting in her thinking of him as "Einstein"—and his wide face seemed impervious to emotional diversity. Her white van passed his house around 7:30 each weekday, and he was consistently stationed in his

5

fenced yard. Khaki pants, light undershirt. Black shoes, black canvas belt. Arms behind back, dog at heels. It was a scenario untinged by weather and revisable by no one. No companions. No people stepping out his front door, or going in. No other car in the driveway besides an old navy-blue Buick Regal that had clearly lost its luster. Front gate and driveway gate never unlocked. Actually, car never moving. Did it even run?

For weeks, this was her morning ritual: stop at the corner on Hill Avenue, glance over at Mr. Einstein. Wait till all the frenetic downhill-coming traffic passed her intersection. Look both ways. Slowly cross Hill. Slow down by Einstein's house. Look at him and see if he returned her gaze. It was crazy, she thought. Seeking—and waiting for!—acknowledgment from an old, nondescript man whose name she did not know. But she could not have avoided this routine, she felt, if she'd wanted to. In the evenings, if the weather was nice and she had energy after her day at work, she'd saunter to her front yard, look to the west toward Einstein's house, and make a mental note of what he was doing, if he happened to be outdoors. Usually, he stood quietly in his yard, gazing at passing traffic, for Hill was a main thoroughfare in that neighborhood. Or Mr. Einstein strolled leisurely in his compact yard, never getting closer than two feet from the fence, never touching his fence. And always the yappy, yippy little furball of a dog bouncing near his ankles. *What was it?*

Though she did not see him gardening, she knew he did, most likely when she was at work. His trees were carefully pruned back, his grass mown, leaves raked. Strangely, there were no flowers in his yard, no shots of color anywhere, only green as far as one could scan: pudgy black pines, spruce bushes near the perimeter of his small house and by his front porch, succulents here and there along the brown wrought iron fence, large echevarrias taking center stage near the front gate. There were no plants in pots, which could have brought color to the landscape. Mr. Einstein's window drapes were always drawn, and heavy metal awnings imposed their drab two-tone stripes on the exteriors of all his windows. She could only imagine how dark the inside of his home must be. She knew these details because she sometimes strolled by his house and up and down the neighboring blocks whenever she had free time in the evenings.

Toward the end of summer, she began waving at the old man when she passed his house on her way to work. At first, he stared at her and did not wave back. After a few days, however, he waved back in a truncated gesture that made her wonder if he'd really waved at her. She smiled at him, nodded politely. He nodded in return and waved once more as she closed her car window and accelerated.

In August, she began waving to him in the afternoons

as well. One late evening, he stood near the corner of his yard, where the fences connected with one another, and watched her white van pass his house on her way home from work. She parked the van in front of her house, as she always did, not liking to park in her narrow driveway where she stored garbage cans and some garden equipment. The old man, standing in his yard with hands clasped behind him, watched her exit the van and walk slowly up her driveway. She turned in time to see him wave at her—and was he smiling?—as she disappeared from his view.

What was it?

She sat at her desk in the evenings, her work sometimes interrupted by musings about the strangeness of this neighbor. Why did she feel compelled to make eye contact, to nod at him in recognition, to wave as she drove by, slow or fast according to her work schedule on any given day? Why did she want, and need, to wave at him—in morning hours or waning daytime—with the eighty yards or so between her and the old man in those afternoon greetings...and with the white van itself between the two of them as she passed by? An old man, a dog seemingly tied to the master's legs, a silence that was almost palpable.

Her work consumed her as the season ended, and her company braced itself for mergers and acquisitions. She could think of little else. The demands, the hours, her associates, the tumult. She could think of little else. Her drive home was increasingly in darkness. Daylight rapidly diminished, and the waning hours became colder. The lavender mountains turned a dark purple, the shadows lining their ribs and their enormous nooks and crannies growing deeper and wider.

As she passed the clapboard house in October gloom, Einstein was rarely in his yard. With fall, days grew shorter, temperatures dropped, and Einstein appeared less and less frequently. But each time she saw him, he stood always in the corner, always at the intersection of the two sections of his chain link fence, the corner of his yard closest to the street. Still unmoving, still looking, still with arms behind his back, the old man watched the van driving by and lifted his arm to acknowledge its passing.

One calm evening, as she drove home in the last minutes of daylight, she noted that Einstein was sans dog. The old man walked the periphery of his fence on this occasion, head never rising, oblivious to her, to the van, to any gestures she may have thrown his way. She pulled into her narrow driveway and wrestled with the grocery bags she needed to balance.

In time, the blades of tawny grass in his yard reached toward the sky. Leaves mounded in orange and rusty piles beneath trailing limbs of the Chinese elm in his front yard. In time, the leaves crinkled and looked like old leather abandoned beneath the tree and scattered under the spruce.

She ceased her occasional walks around the block as obligations sucked more and more hours from her calendars. Frequently arriving home very late from work, she couldn't have guessed if Mr. Einstein stood in his front yard to greet her anymore. Ultimately, she realized one night with a loud sigh, she didn't care.

When the Buick went absent, she took a walk past his house one more time, just to be sure. Nothing. Silence. A vacuum. She recalled the airplane they'd both seen, that primal connection neither ever discussed.

Before the end of the week, she began using another route to work each morning.

The Heavens Weep for Us

Neighbors and brothers and sisters and fathers and mothers meld together in common pain. Both caskets are small.

The Heavens Weep for Us

They close ranks quickly, gray, pregnant banks of clouds not so high above our heads. The wind waves its wispy fingers behind trees, atop hills, in blue valleys and ridges, through crevices and slopes. Creeks puff their little bosoms and prepare to fill. God's little orchestra, syncopated, humming, thrumming, building, building until tears spill.

Black umbrellas clump together, edges wavy with dotted water. Neighbors and brothers and sisters and fathers and mothers meld together in common pain. Both caskets are small, mere plain boxes hobbled together with moans and prayers and whys. Side by side, they could've been children's toy boxes brimming with bears and puppets. But they sit on dirt now, bare pine streaked orange with rivulets of rain.

It's one wound in the earth, just one gape waiting patiently to be filled. One wound smaller than the usual, ashamed to swallow tiny coffins, preferring to be sated with a ripe old soul. But the baby caskets swinging on ropes slowly settle on the bottom, clicking on rocks and dusty stones, the two boxes touching sides, lying together, ready to be tucked in.

Stars fallen.

Moonbeams shamed.

Thunder should have alarmed the town: "Here, here, over here! Hear, hear!"

But the heavens were silent that night.

Silence same as silence old. Silence of the years, of neighbors choosing silence over truth, uncles choosing silence over courage, cousins choosing silence over conflict. Little children of the broken bones, tiny faces of the bloodied lips, slender shoulders with holes burnt in. Little children of the dirt. Little children blued and purpled, reddened and bumpy.

Little silent children in a silent watching village.

Flames licked the moon. Smoke curled into misty darkness too ashamed to swallow it. Wood crackled and heaved and buckled and smothered hope. Two swaddled lumps in the corner, under their mattress, clinging together, calling.

Does it matter that their ma was frightened of him? Torn by his knuckles, hands large like iron bellows, frightened of his whiskey-breath and wide leather belt? Does it matter that she left?

Does it matter he survived? Clinking glasses at the tavern, readying his hands for her at home, licking lips while flames licked his sons. And their mother not there, not knowing. Fickle moon not telling.

Stars fallen.

Moonbeams shamed.

But the heavens weep today, tears late, tears slow, silence interred.

The heavens weep for us.

Little Box

You could be the one, Petra nodded to herself. You could be the one who owned the little green box, who took out whatever beautiful jewelry was in it, who then tossed it out for me to find.

Little Box

The little box caught her eye as she walked her daughter's dog down the narrow sidewalk in the alley. She almost walked past the little treasure, thrown as it was on the ground near the trash bins. But it was open, lying face-up, its smooth emerald leatherette skin dusty from lying on the ground in a tiny patch of crabgrass. She pulled hard on the large dog's leash to get its attention and get it to stop awhile. She picked up the empty box. Yes, that's what she thought it said: *Neiman Marcus*. The graceful golden script was stamped across the cream-colored satin lining the lid. Creamy velvet lined the bottom in a fancy two-part flap that closed on itself. It was a hinged jewelry box, the kind bearing a lovely ring or a pair of earrings, a gold chain, or anything precious enough to package in a small surprise that could be tucked proudly, protectively into a man's coat pocket or a woman's purse.

She held the little box in her palm, unknowingly smiling as she gazed at it. She shook it firmly, dust swirling away almost invisibly, and rubbed it against her pant leg. Almost pristine! *Neiman Marcus.* She stood entranced, imagining the gift that had once lain inside, impressed with its unseen beauty but confident that it was undoubtedly costly and elegant. *Lucky, lucky recipient*, she thought.

She looked closely around the spot where the box had lain, seeing if perhaps its contents had dropped out accidentally. Perhaps someone had stolen the jewelry, maybe in a house burglary, and had been scared or surprised, had had to flee the scene quickly and had thrown it here, perhaps thinking to return later, in darkness, to retrieve it. Maybe, then, whatever had been in the box had fallen out and might still be lying on the ground nearby. She crouched close to the ground and peered into the darkness beneath the trash bin. Bare dirt there, nothing else. She ran her free hand slowly, methodically over the sparse grass in the spot where she'd found the little box. She adjusted her eyeglasses, blinked to clear her vision, and stooped close to the ground. Nothing. She noticed that an empty cardboard box and scrunched-up gift bag lay nearby. Rising slowly, she sighed and dusted herself. She decided that her little box had spilled out of the bin along with the other detritus. Whoever the owner, the recipient of the jewelry, was, she'd probably just overstuffed the bin.

The Heavens Weep for Us

The dog was lying on the ground, pensive, waiting. She yanked on the leash once, and he followed her obediently the rest of the way home.

Petra was visiting her daughter in Chicago. She'd been in the city for almost two weeks now, and her daughter, Celeste, had been ecstatic that her mother had found time, in her recent retirement from retail sales in Arizona, to visit her. Celeste had been married for five years to an utterly handsome, polished man named Trino, and the two had decided to remain childless. It was best for their careers, they had decided. So Celeste, an attorney, and Trino, a top-level computer management company executive, were the consummate professional couple, both high achievers who didn't miss the proverbial patter of little feet in their Chicago condominium. Their condo, situated in the southern portion of the city's famous North Shore district, reflected their refined tastes and love of luxury.

"You didn't get lost today, did you, Mom?" Celeste called good-naturedly from the balcony as Petra and Mica, the family Labrador, opened the front door. Celeste already had wine glass in hand, her bare feet resting on the bottom rail of the iron balcony. The view from here was spectacular, and Celeste often spent the first hour or so of her arrival home from work sitting on her twentieth-floor balcony, watching the last lights of the day settle on the sailboats in the marina nearby.

"Thanks for your faith in me," Petra replied with equal good humor. Since her arrival, Petra had insisted upon walking the dog, who was taken out four times a day to do his duties. So far, Petra had twice lost her way on these walks, preferring the narrow, winding residential streets rather than the bustling boulevards that seemed to surround her daughter's home. Petra unleashed Mica and reached into her pants pocket for the little jewelry box. She stood silently in the darkened foyer gazing at the box and decided that it was best not to tell Celeste that she'd retrieved the box by a trash bin in an alley. Instead, as she passed the polished walnut console next to the living room doorway, Petra placed the little box in the single drawer, safely out of sight but near enough for her to remember to put it in her suitcase later tonight.

She paused in the kitchen just long enough to pour herself a glass of iced tea. She used one of her daughter's fine wine glasses and felt luxurious as she settled herself onto the *chaise longue* next to her daughter.

"So where's Trino?" asked Petra. She knew he usually came home later than did Celeste, but tonight he seemed to be extra late.

"The question of the hour," said Celeste, her mood changing slightly. She reached for the cell phone on the small table next to her and checked her messages. "Usually he calls to tell me where he is and approximately when he'll be home. *Nada* today. *Nada*." She shrugged her shoulders and took a sip of wine. She turned to look at Petra and shrugged again.

"Well, he's a very busy man," said Petra as reassuringly as she could. She looked away from her daughter, focusing instead on the white caps that were starting to whip up across Lake Michigan as she sipped her tea. Petra noticed, as she did each evening, how the fading light of day blurred the distinction between the rocking surface of the water and the graying sky.

Alone in the guest room that night, Petra felt restless. She'd missed Trino's company at the dinner table tonight. Always attentive and courteous, Trino was every mother's dream for her daughter. Well-educated, brilliant, ambitious, successful. Not arrogant, no, not ever. Not condescending, as others as successful as he might be. Not boastful of his success. Modest to the core. Hard-luck kid, she'd heard. East Los Angeles, deep in the barrio. Immigrants. Gangs. He'd seen them, lived them, been them. Garfield High School scholar. Berkeley. The hard knocks and the accolades always flowed in a stream side by side when she thought about her only son-in-law and how lucky, how blessed Celeste was to have won Trino's heart.

So tonight was hard for her. When she and Celeste finally heard the key turn in the lock, there was mutual relief and mutual irritation. They'd both turned to the clock on the mantel, then to a noticeably-weary Trino as he'd carefully closed the heavy door behind him and placed his briefcase inside the foyer closet. He smiled faintly, walked softly to his wife and kissed her on the cheek, then kissed Petra on the forehead, calling her "Mama." Always the gentleman, the good son. It was hard to be angry at such a gentle soul.

But not for Celeste. Her iciness was just this side of palpable. She'd opened her mouth to speak, then had glanced at her mother. Petra understood and wished them a good night. The murmuring voices had begun as soon as her bedroom door had closed. She couldn't make out any of the words and would not have wanted to know, in any case. Petra prepared for bed, the muffled voices on the other side of the walls rising and falling, rising and falling, like the rolling waters of the lake beyond their balcony.

The greatest redeemer is a new day. A new allocation of twenty-four hours, starting with dazzling slants of light hitting the rug, the walls, the bedcoverings in irresistible bursts of optimism. Who can resist? The freshness outside beckons. The blue clarity above the windows challenges the blue of the lake to be bluer, more inviting. Standing on the balcony, breathing in the unsullied promise of a clean start, Petra was uplifted and caught herself humming a tune she had sung on her honeymoon forty years ago. She smiled to herself as she readied for the new day.

At breakfast, Celeste and Trino also seemed renewed. Whatever had come between them last night wasn't present in the room anymore. Petra was relieved and happy. Petra hummed the old honeymoon tune again and related to the young couple how she and her new husband had danced to that tune again and again, putting the old LP on the turntable repeatedly, spinning and turning in their Santa Barbara hotel room until daylight.

I wish you bluebirds in the spring, a happy song to make you sing. I wish you health, I wish you wealth, I wish you love. And in July a lemonade to cool you in some leafy glade. I wish you health, I wish you wealth, I wish you love.

"It was a sad song, actually," said Petra, as she recalled the final stanzas. She fell pensive. "But it was so romantic, so full of feeling, of love. Your daddy and I felt it in our souls."

Celeste wended her way around the huge kitchen island and wrapped her arms around her mother's shoulders. She reached for her briefcase on a nearby stool and leaned over to kiss Petra's cheek.

"You always called it, Mom, always called the shots right. If anyone knows love, it's you."

"Amen, amen," said Trino cheerfully. He balanced his

coffee mug in one hand and car keys in the other. He kissed his mother-in-law on the cheek and hurried after Celeste, their briefcases banging together briefly as each playfully tried to go through the front door first.

Petra couldn't help herself. With Trino and Celeste at work all day—and both their workdays were invariably long—she had many hours alone. Luckily for her, she loved Chicago, or at least the part of the city she knew: the historic Old Town Triangle, Lincoln Park, Sheffield, Millenium Park, Grant Park, the Gold Coast. An Arizona girl used to dry hills and cactus, to Wal-Mart and Target, where she'd launched and ended her retail career, can appreciate the niceties of a world-class city. Healthy and vibrant in retirement, Petra walked the beautiful districts of Chicago, occasionally hailing a cab or hopping on the El to cover more territory. The sparkling storefronts on Michigan Avenue, with their colorful banners of all shapes and sizes suspended from long, shining poles and flapping in the notorious Chicago wind, fascinated her. Another walking destination close to Petra's heart, if not her daughter's condo, were the historic row houses on Crilly Place in Old Town, architectural gems all. None of these escaped her attention, her appreciation. She was vicariously living the life of her child.

On the last full day in town, Petra revisited the place

where she'd found the little green box. She wasn't walking
Mica that day. She wanted to explore at her pace, not the
dog's. She studied the houses on the street: bold brick
homes shoulder to shoulder with other slender homes, some
stone, some wood, many a combination of textures and ma-
terials, all with window boxes spilling flowers of every
color and variety, with wide, high staircases leading to
front doors often at the second floor level. The pocket gar-
dens surrounded by wrought iron railings neatly painted a
glossy black or shiny brown belied the grandeur of stained-
glass windows, or beveled leaded glass, and imposing tur-
rets with complicated brick work. Petra wished she'd studied architecture in school.

"Poor people don't live here," she whispered to herself.
Neiman Marcus could live here. Neiman Marcus' box came
here, she added silently. Whoever received that jewelry box
and its contents was a high-class person who probably already had such high-class jewelry and knew the high-class
store well.

As Petra passed near the spot where she'd found the little box, a young woman was locking her front door. The
woman, very slender and with long, lustrous dark hair, almost bumped into Petra as she swirled down her stairs.
Petra caught sight of her smooth face and bright lips as she
excused herself and slipped past the older woman. The
young woman could have been a fashion model, or an ac-

tress. Petra turned discreetly to stare at the woman's retreating figure.

You could be the one, Petra nodded to herself. *You could be the one who owned the little green box, who took out whatever beautiful jewelry was in it, who then tossed it out for me to find.*

Petra did not take the little box on the airplane with her. She was exiting the Phoenix airport when she realized she'd forgotten it in the console drawer in Celeste's foyer. She was crestfallen. By the time she reached her home on the outskirts of the city, Petra was downright angry at herself. That Neiman Marcus box was something special. Not only was it a charming souvenir of her trip to visit her beloved daughter, but it was something she could have used.

Since her retirement, Petra had supplemented her modest pension with estate sales. She cleaned people's homes when they remodeled, relocated, or died. She organized and sold their belongings, charging a respectable fee for her services. Sometimes she augmented the merchandise with her own second-hand finds from area flea markets, local thrift shops and yard sales. Sometimes she added discards from her own closets and cupboards or even from things she'd find left out on the curb for anyone to take. It always amazed Petra that people could be wasteful, and things she'd find streetside as she went about her business sometimes astounded her: an oak desk chair one time; a large beveled closet door mirror on another occasion; a gorgeous wrought iron garden gate last month. Waste not, want not, she believed. The little green box was to be part of her jewelry display paraphernalia. Petra owned glass display cases, small tables, petite stands with spokes for hanging necklaces. She was, after all, a businesswoman, an estate sale consultant, despite how dusty and dirty her work could get.

Celeste did not know all this. Petra felt uncomfortable letting her daughter know how she needed to supplement her pension. And after seeing now for a couple of years how her daughter lived in Chicago, meeting the high-society friends in Celeste's circle, knowing how Trino valued his ascent into respectable society...no, there was no way Celeste or Trino would ever know that she, Petra, dealt with people's castoffs.

Definitely, Petra would say nothing to her daughter about the dusty little green box she'd picked up in an alley near a trash bin.

It was insidiously slow, but it was insidious nonetheless. Celeste's marriage was dying. Signs of its unraveling came to Petra's attention about two months after her Chicago visit. First an email: Celeste suspected Trino was seeing someone. Cryptic, emotionless, the email stunned Petra. She did not respond, hoping that it was just another fight, another misunderstanding, maybe like the one she'd partially witnessed during her trip to Chicago. Could Trino have changed so much in such little time? It couldn't be so.

Then the phone calls: Trino was often very late coming home. Celeste was hesitant at first to report this to her mother. She seemed apologetic for venting. But it wasn't just venting. It was a broken heart speaking its truth.

Then despair swirled together, and its arc embraced all channels: pained emails; long, slow phone conversations when Celeste was alone at home and didn't know where her husband was; a few angry, spiteful letters probably written at work, when Celeste's hurt precluded productivity, but the office precluded full disclosure of her pain. Petra was devastated. She simply couldn't respond, didn't know how to respond. Celeste's despair became Petra's, but the mother's disbelief was a vessel of deep hurt unto itself.

How could Trino do this? How could he have transformed himself from a model husband into a monster? Petra could not fathom this and thus didn't take sides in the unraveling. She carried on with her life in Arizona, but her spirit was in Chicago, where the freshness and beauty of a vibrant city couldn't ameliorate the destitute condition of her child's life.

Ultimately, the resolution was a double-edged sword: the end came somewhat swiftly and stanched the suffering, but the end was the end, and the end to something that was once so wonderful can never be a happy thing. Celeste showed up at Petra's door in the fifth month of her discontent. She and Trino were divorcing. With her daughter before her eyes, with the full-blown view of her child's pain not distant anymore, Petra's numbness dissolved. She and Celeste settled in for a long heart-to-heart, possibly for a dissection of a union that had been meant to last forever.

Petra finally summoned the courage to ask what she'd been unable to believe: "What was it that alerted you?" She didn't need to phrase it any other way.

Celeste was calm.

"I found evidence," she said.

"Evidence? Evidence of what?"

"Evidence that there was someone else," Celeste replied, still calm, "despite the fact that for months he kept denying and denying."

"*For months*'?" repeated Petra. "Did he finally confess?"

Celeste glanced at her mother then gazed out the window. "No. Not confessed. Never." She looked again at her mother. "He chose silence. Just shut me out. Shut out the truth. He just chose silence."

"But how could you be sure your evidence was … that?"

"I knew. I just knew."

Petra was still incredulous.

"What exactly did you find?"

Celeste shifted on the sofa in the stifling living room. The door was wide open, and it was after midnight. The air was still suffocating.

"He bought expensive jewelry for another woman…"

Petra held her breath.

"…from Neiman Marcus," continued Celeste. "I found the little green box he'd placed it in. He never even had the courage to admit it when I confronted him with it."

Petra could hardly breathe. She rose slowly from the sofa.

"You found it in the console in the foyer," she said to Celeste. Celeste nodded, surprised.

"How did you…." Celeste started and stopped.

Petra had collapsed, weeping inconsolably, onto the floor.

Marry Me

"Marry me," she said once again. She did not smile, did not avert her gaze. Diego was silent then stared at his feet as he shuffled before responding.

Marry Me

1

He couldn't believe his ears. He looked around slowly, trying to figure out who had spoken to him. He had never been in the small neighborhood market before, being somewhat new to Laredo, so he wasn't familiar with the layout of the place. It was dimly-lit and crowded with shelves placed near each other, making the aisles narrow and difficult to navigate. Who had spoken to him? And was it to him?

"Pardon me?" he said in a low voice as he continued to scan the small store. He noticed that he was the only customer, so whoever had spoken had most likely addressed him.

Silence. He could hear someone's breathing before the voice called out to him from the semi-darkness again.

"Marry me."

It was a woman's voice. It came from the corner, partly shielded by a tall rack of Fritos and potato chips. Diego walked slowly in the direction of the voice and craned his neck to see behind the rack.

An old woman rocked slowly in an aluminum rocker. Diego guessed she was about eighty years old, and he wondered if she'd really gotten a good look at him. Diego had just celebrated his twenty-second birthday before moving to Laredo to fend for his widowed mother, so he wasn't exactly a right match for the old lady in the chair. He smiled faintly as he pointed to his chest.

"Pardon me? Are you addressing me?" He looked around again then tried to see into the back room, whose doorway stood directly behind the old woman. Apparently no one else was present. It was just him and the old lady.

The woman continued rocking rhythmically, her gaze never leaving Diego's face. Though her face and exposed hands and arms gave ample testament to many decades of existence on earth, her hair was remarkably black, probably through the aid of a bottle, thought Diego. She wore lipstick, a subtle shade, and long, looping silver earrings. Her dark green shawl enveloped her torso tightly, and Diego was reminded briefly of Indian papooses. The woman's leathered face was certainly as dark as an Indian's.

"Marry me," she said once again. She did not smile, did

not avert her gaze. Diego was silent then stared at his feet as he shuffled before responding.

"I need to pay you for this merchandise." He held forth a loaf of bread, two cans of sodas, and a small package of oatmeal cookies.

"*Te amo. Cázate conmigo.*" Her voice was strong, sure of itself. *I love you. Marry me.*

Diego placed a ten-dollar bill on the counter near the old woman and hurried out into the searing sunlight.

2

Marta, Diego's mother, had suffered a heart attack ten days after she'd buried her husband, who himself had succumbed to a massive coronary. After staying in a local convalescent hospital for almost three months, Marta had been sent home by her doctor with the admonition that she needed to "reinvent" herself.

"Get a life," he told her. "You're not dead. You beat death. That's a sign from God that you've got to grab the bull by the horns and go for the gusto!" He seemed unembarrassed by his triteness. Marta couldn't tell if he was merely being condescending toward her—*gringo* doctor that he was—or if he simply wasn't very bright. And what on earth did the idiot mean by "reinvent"? She wasn't a product, or a piece of technology. She was a human being!

This she retold with great relish to Diego when he had arrived at her side recently. The sight of her only child—a strapping, handsome man who'd put his life on hold to tend to her—had almost wiped away the memory of her husband's final days of suffering. A recent college graduate in Virginia, Diego had left his girlfriend behind with promises to return by the end of the year, had refused three job offers from vaunted companies in Virginia, and had already begun familiarizing himself with Laredo, a town so alien to him with its red dust, ramshackle neighborhoods, interminable heat, and congenital identity crisis. He was certainly trying to understand.

Or was he?

"Son," she said to him one day. "What's the latest with Kika?" *Kika* was short for *Francisca*. Francisca was the eighty-year-old woman who had proposed to Diego.

Diego rolled his eyes but said nothing. He continued folding laundry on the kitchen table, took a swig from his coffee mug, then sighed.

"What's to report, Mom? That I can't ever go into that store without her ogling me and asking me to marry her? That I've tried a dozen times to laugh it off? That she doesn't care who's listening or watching when she harasses me like that?"

"Harass?" said Marta. "Why do you say she's harassing you?"

"Women can harass men, you know," he snorted. "I feel like the proverbial piece of meat. She doesn't laugh or smile or giggle, chuckle, or anything that might make it look like a joke. In fact," he paused for effect, "*I'm* the joke!"

"Why should she make you, or anyone else, think she's joking?" asked Marta. "She wants to marry you."

Diego stared at his mother. She looked calmly at him. He couldn't believe it. He had two looney old women on his hands.

3

Kika had not seen Diego for almost three weeks now. As she locked her store for the night, she recalled the day he'd come to town, long heralded by her old acquaintance Marta. Though Marta was almost twenty years her junior, and was just an occasional friend of hers, she'd long known Marta and her husband. They were an amicable couple, well-respected in their neighborhood not only for their many years of residency, but for their good deeds through church, and their willingness to help out whenever any neighbor needed help, which, in their dusty, working-class neighborhood, was frequent. The husband had been a good man, successful in business, choosing to stay in the neighborhood out of loyalty to his roots. This loyalty was nothing small, nothing small in the eyes of Laredo people, Laredo poor people. As she tested the doorknob of her store's front door, Kika cursed, under her breath, the heart attack that had killed Marta's husband.

She remembered Diego as a boy. Diego the smart boy, the one who went to a private academy far from Laredo. Diego the smart boy, the one who went to a faraway high school instead of taking a job in town to support his family. Diego the smart boy who went far, far away to college, the first in their neighborhood to do so. Diego the boy who turned into a man…a beautiful man.

Kika's old heart beat faster at the thought, too fast for an old woman. She took several deep breaths before she allowed herself to picture how Diego looked that first day he'd walked into her store four months ago: tall, beautiful, smart. In the dim light, his entrance had literally taken her breath away. When he'd stopped a few steps inside her front door, turned sideways to inspect the fruit, and bent over slightly to check the price, she'd stared at him incredulously. The shadows hit his face, his hair, his shoulders in such a way, that….

Kika couldn't bear the thought. She shut her eyes tightly, pressed her fingers into her eyelids to make the picture go away.

4

What an inconvenience! They needed a quart of milk. That's all: a quart of milk. Diego knew Kika's store had it, and it was only three blocks away from his mother's home, but he couldn't bear the thought of going there. The only time he'd been the lone customer was that fateful first day. Ever since then, there had been others—men, women, children, and everything in between—that would hear Kika propose to him shamelessly. It was always the same, she sitting in the corner in her rocker, in the shadows, never taking her eyes off him, speaking to him in a clear, firm voice, asking him (no, not asking but *telling* him) to marry her.

"Diego, marry me. You know I love you. I want to marry you." Always serious. Always calm-faced. Never flinching despite the customers' reactions, or Diego's.

As the weeks ground forward, it became increasingly more irritating to Diego to endure the snickers, chuckles, and sometimes outright guffaws of the other customers, some of whom would goad him by yelling inanities like, "Go for it, man!" The older men would often smile sardonically, glancing sideways at the woman they themselves could not imagine romancing. The younger people simply didn't care to be discreet. Their laughter was raucous.

In his first couple of weeks in Laredo, Diego had attempted to defuse the teasing with light comedy. He'd smile broadly, making kissing gestures toward the old woman in the corner. He'd wink knowingly, jiggle his eyebrows upward, hand-blow kisses to Kika, and once, even shook his hips in mock lechery. But he couldn't maintain this charade for long. His entire life, he'd been protected from the rough edges of Laredo, had been spirited away to places that enabled him to grow smooth and clear like a pebble rounded perfectly by strong water. Diego was neither a lecher nor a credible pretender to lechery. Very quickly, he became himself, and himself was a beautiful, smart young man repulsed by an eighty-year-old woman's advances and the salacious reactions of enablers. So Diego began ignoring her words, and he'd shuffle to the counter, show her his purchases, pay quickly, and duck out with as much dignity as he could salvage.

As the weeks passed, however, salvation became more difficult. He became the butt of jokes beyond Kika's market. He was "Kika's Honey," or "Francisca's *Favorito*" in places outside her borders: in other places of commerce, in church, parking lots, street corners, living rooms. Even people who forged friendships with Diego commented on how fervently Kika wanted him and ribbed him about his magical powers of geriatric attraction.

What a bummer! Again, (for how many weeks now?) Diego would have to go somewhere else for milk.

5

Marta couldn't believe it. The idiot doctor was right. She *could* "reinvent" herself and was actually doing so. Doing so pretty well, thank you. She'd had to buy an appointment book, though she preferred to call it just a calendar. She'd spend her mornings, while Diego ran errands for her, writing small notes in the blocks of days lined with gilt edging. A lunch meeting here, a medical appointment there. Some light shopping on this day, then a lunch date (she always hesitated when using the word "date") there. At first Marta's little black scribbles took little space from the blocks, but, with the weeks sliding by since Diego's arrival, more and more ink made its presence felt within her gilt-lined pages. She had gotten a life, as the doctor had urged.

In the evenings, while Diego read in his room or relaxed with friends in the living room, Marta took to entertaining male friends of her own in the den or sometimes in her well-appointed patio, tiki torches blazing, oldies crooning from hidden speakers. In time, Marta took wine glasses out of storage and scheduled dinner parties. After all, her rehabilitation had gone on schedule...no, had *surpassed* the scheduled milestones. With her doctors' meticulous ministerings, Marta had embarked on a proverbial new chapter as a stronger, happier (yes, happier) woman.

Diego overheard his mother on the phone one morning:

"Yes, it is amazing, isn't it? I was on the brink of death. Yes, yes. I do. I give all the credit to my son. Yes, I do. He came here to rescue me."

Wordlessly, Diego came around the kitchen counter, embraced his mother, and blinked rapidly as he thought about how much he wanted her to be happy.

6

It had been a difficult month for Kika. She had not gone to her store for almost two weeks now. Luckily, her youngest brother had been able to open the store each day and tend it till closing time. He'd done so without complaints and thus had eased Kika's guilt about pulling him away from his own job. His sons had covered for him at the gardening firm where they all worked together.

It had always been this way, or so it seemed to Kika: all her family working together for their communal good. Kika's husband had bought the store with savings he'd brought with them from Mexico and had reveled in the fact that their native land and adopted land co-existed side by side. Side by side. That was the beauty of Laredo. Never did Kika or her husband feel that they had abandoned their motherland for this newer, richer place called America. The border was practically no border at all, its permeability allowing Kika and her family the luxury of not giving up the old ways. Their loyalties straddled the Rio Grande.

Kika had married young, at sixteen, the youngest of seven daughters. Her husband-to-be had fallen in love with the slender girl when he first saw her on her father's horse, cantering toward the village market, her thick black hair bouncing behind her shoulders and on the saddle of the horse, the slender girl slowing the horse into a gentle trot as she entered the heart of the village. When she arrived, dismounted from the mare, and walked toward where he and his family sold tomatoes in giant handwoven baskets, she entered his heart as well. This girl, this girl named Francisca, would be his wife.

When they came across the border for the store, for their dreams, for a new life, they were halfway done with theirs, really. She was fifty years old already, set in her ways, the old-country ways, ways she could never and would never discard. She was set in her love of him, her deep, deep love of him, which she could never and would never discard. Kika stayed married to her husband for fifty-four years, till a heart attack killed him and killed her, too. In the decade since his death, tending their store by herself helped her to remain strong, to remember why they'd come across the border, to remember why she still awoke each day and went through the machinations of pretending to be alive.

And then *he* walked into their store, her store. The tall,

smart, beautiful Diego. The Diego with the sunlight and shadows hitting his face and neck and shoulders just so. The Diego with the head and hair and jaw that she always adored, since she was sixteen. The Diego with the looks of the man she'd caressed, kissed, and adored for fifty-four years.

She knew Marta's boy would never marry her. For this she'd been prepared. She wasn't braced for the pain of losing her husband twice.

Comatose

It was a hell of an accident. How she survived was well beyond his comprehension, anybody's comprehension.

Comatose

I

Such a pity. These cases were always hard for him, no matter who the people were, how old they were, what had turned their little worlds upside down. And it never got easier. When they were young like this one, a mother with a small child at home—well, it tested his composure more than he liked to acknowledge.

He sighed as he approached Room 324. He reached for the file folder on the door, stood outside the room as he flipped wearily through the day's notes: blood pressure, temperature, anecdotes about Paula's lack of responsiveness. He snorted. *Lack of responsiveness?* Of course.

Paula was lucky to be alive. Or maybe not.

Not lucky. Not really alive.

It was a hell of an accident. How she survived was well

beyond his comprehension, anybody's comprehension. How she was brought into his hospital with her body in one piece, how her face was recognizable as human, how she'd been able to open her eyes on the gurney as they wheeled her into the trauma unit, how she'd squeezed his hand before the operation. One hell of a twisted, searing, crushing accident, they all told him, the police, paramedics, all the shell-shocked people who'd been there, who'd cut her loose from what should've been her metal tomb, who rushed her through the double doors with tremulous faith, urgent faith.

Dr. Ignacio closed her folder, then slowly pushed the door open.

Even after thirty years on the hospital staff, these things never got any easier for him.

II

When Paula's husband, Robert, got the call after midnight that Sunday night, he'd bundled Richie in the nearest blanket he could find and rushed him to the next door neighbors' house. Miraculously, his little boy never woke and only muttered momentarily when his father passed him into the frightened arms of his neighbors. They were good people, had babysat Richie in the past, and would do anything for Paula and her husband. They stared at Robert with mouths agape, unable to fully decipher his grief–babble but clearly understanding that something horrendous had happened to Paula and that he had to go now.

How Robert made it to the hospital in one piece was a minor miracle. He wept all the way. He ran red lights— streets were deserted at that time anyway—and turned corners on two wheels and prayers. At the hospital, no nurse, no orderly could quell his turmoil, but when the police eventually arrived to speak with him, they spoke to stone. Robert didn't see them, didn't really hear them. He was a stricken man whose eyes were already seeing past the stoic police faces, whose ears were already attuned to messages beyond the earnest mouths of these protectors. He seemed to be looking into the bloody room upstairs where Paula lay at that moment, fighting for her life, unaware that Robert had also just begun to fight for his.

When, many hours later, Paula was wheeled into Room 324, bandaged and comatose, Robert likewise fell still. This petite lump of gauze, yards and yards of enwrapped hope, the closed eyes barely visible between straps of white circling her face and body, was his wife, Richie's mother, the woman in whose arms he'd once planned to die as a withered man ages hence.

This couldn't be happening.

III

Robert never left Paula's side.

I'm still here, my darling. Hold my hand and don't cry anymore. Please hear me.

Silence, or near-silence. Only the occasional sound of sniffling. Sometimes there were others in the room. Even after all these days—or weeks? months?—they kept coming. Bless their hearts. They kept coming. Some read aloud. Some whispered their torment to one another.

Torment? What do you know of torment, my loved ones?

Some prayed, more than one voice, holding hands it seemed. The priest from her childhood church with his voice tinny and fervent. Some visitors to her bedside read softly, determinedly, never running out of material to share. Books, newspapers, letters. All the same: messages of hope, perseverance, courage, love amidst darkness. They stole the words of others to give voice to their own fears. Fear of giving up, of becoming too busy to care anymore, of forgetting loyalty and its promises. In the daily bustling in her room, the goings and comings, Paula lay unmoving, eyes sealed, but it seemed sometimes that her life was being replayed with her lying by helplessly.

Don't despair. I know your love.

And always Robert's voice as a backdrop, or alone

when visitors had left. Robert's voice tired but brave, or beaten and fearful, soothing her, trying to delve through the awful speechlessness, seeking her soul beneath the bandages, trying to connect with whatever immortality had survived the crash.

You're here, my love, as weary as I am, but you're here.

And sometimes Robert's voice, alone, indecipherable, guilty and shamed, unquestionably shamed.

I understand. I know the answer. You didn't have to say it.

IV

He shouldn't have let her leave that night. He shouldn't have. He shouldn't have left her questions unanswered, shouldn't have done what he did. There were so many "shouldn't haves" swirling in his gut.

"But do you still love her?" she'd asked.

Robert ignored his wife at first, changed channels aimlessly. He was far away as usual. There but not there. Feet on the scarred table, the one they'd built together when they first moved into the house. Cold beer nearby, newspaper, papers from work, remote control: the usual detritus of his day, the accoutrements of his evening. He listened momentarily to the newscast, the weather report, yawned, and surfed the channels again. When she repeated her question, this time moving into the living room doorway, he knew he'd have to respond.

He glanced in her direction. "Don't know," he said flatly.

"How can you not know?" she persisted. She was wiping a platter dry, and she was crying. Her face was very pink and shimmered in the lamplight near the doorway. But he didn't see, and her voice was even.

He lowered the volume on the TV but continued half-listening to the weather report: heavy rains. He thought fleetingly of finding the cat and bringing her in. Cats. What the hell; they always manage anyway. They ignore most humans and don't really need them, except for feedings. Damn the cat. She could withstand the rains. He yawned again.

"Do you? Do you still love her…or see her?"

She was squatting in front of him now, dishes all done for the night, dishtowel still in her hand. She put her face in front of his, blocked the TV. He had to look at her, had to see the tears, the puffed eyes, smeared makeup. Damn it. Why couldn't she be like the cat?

Or like…*her.*

His *other* "her." The one who filled his hours when he needed the filling. The one with the slippery laugh, fast eyes, and a bottomless, insatiable appetite. The one no man could lay claim to, really. She chose you, had her fun with you, made you feel like you couldn't live without her, but she could live without you. Strong, independent, didn't have to know if you loved her or not. The one Paula asked about right now: the one tearing her up, the one who used to sit at her dinner table, who used to go running along the lake with her, the one who used to be the surrogate sister, for her, for him.

Robert looked at Paula but didn't understand. Didn't understand how their "sister" could have transformed so easily into...

He looked at his wife and searched for words, searched for some understanding of what had happened to Paula, what had happened to him, what had happened to *her*. He fished in his mind lazily at first, then—as he stared at Paula's swollen face—guilt made him feel obligated to find words to explain what had happened in their marriage. But words were absent.

Robert sighed, held Paula's weeping face in his hands, and shook his head. He didn't know. He truly didn't know. Did he love her? Love Paula? Love *her*? He didn't understand and truly didn't know. He shook his head again and looked at last at his feet. That was all he could summon. Shame enough to hang his head momentarily and stare at his feet, totally at a loss for words.

That's when Paula rose quietly and dropped the dishcloth on her husband's lap. She smiled down at him. Smiled sweetly, he was astounded to see. He smiled back. Maybe she understood after all, somehow understood. She rattled through the keys in the bowl by the front door and, again wordlessly, walked briskly out the door into the heavy rains.

V

Dr. Ignacio had returned to the nurse's station at the hospital after tending to his regular patients in his office across town. He sat in the cramped cubicle across from Paula's room and reviewed her brain scans again. It was late, the hospital corridors long, cold mazes that echoed any footsteps much more loudly than in the daytime. Two nurses worked quietly near the desk where Dr. Ignacio sat, their faces lit mainly by their computer screens. Paula's room, and the others, stood as darkened doorways up and down the line.

A portion of Paula's brain had been crushed in the accident. Enough had been unharmed to allow her to remain alive, but nothing so far—not the surgery or any other interventions—had changed the fact that Paula would probably never regain consciousness. Dr. Ignacio put the scans and the paperwork down, rubbed his forehead slowly, and decided he needed another cup of coffee.

The Heavens Weep for Us

Medicine has come a long way, he thought. In decades past, Paula would have died in her mangled car. But now she, and her family, lived in limbo. Such a pity that someone young, and, by all accounts, the center of a loving, thriving little family, should lie now in...

Dr. Ignacio paused here, took a sip of coffee. He detested the phrase and cursed whoever had coined it long ago. "Persistent vegetative state." To see a human being encased in a shell of speechlessness and immobility, lacking vitality, but with body still warm, heart still beating, lungs still extending and distending, eyes sometimes still opening...well, to call such a being a vegetable had always offended his sense of humanity. What, really, does medicine know? Is there really no human consciousness in that crushed brain? How can medicine track, or even identify, the spark of life that keeps someone like Paula alive? Has medicine really come so far as to even claim it can do that?

A human spark?

Dr. Ignacio groaned as he rose from the desk. He lifted his eyeglasses to the top of his forehead and rubbed the bridge of his nose, absorbed in thought. The nurses had left the station momentarily, so he was alone in the semi-darkness for a few minutes. He gazed at Paula's darkened doorway. His biggest struggle was not knowing: knowing that doctors didn't have all the answers, obviously, but not knowing how, or if, anyone in Paula's condition could have a spark he'd term "life." Not knowing if there really was anything not physiologically identified that could and did sustain life. Not knowing if he wished Paula continued in her limbo-life, or if he wished she'd let go.

Not always knowing when and where life ends, really.

VI

They'd been unbelievably happy for the first five years. Everyone said they couldn't believe what a great couple Paula and Robert were, couldn't believe how much in love they looked. "Radiant," some would say. "Lucky in love," the neighbors would tell them. Then, when Richie, purple and crinkled and the most beautiful newborn Paula and Robert could imagine, entered their world, his grandparents prophesied great fortune for him for being born into such a union. Lucky, lucky little Richie, to have such in-love parents! What child could wish for more?

Trivialities have immense power. Centuries of floods and storms wear away mammoth cliffs and mountains, shrink icebergs, carve canyons from granite. Friendly, gurgling water shrinks large rocks into small, smooth pebbles glistening timidly in clear creek waters. People marvel at the mega power of the smoothest rivers, the clearest rains, the softest snow as they transform giants into flattened beds and plateaus, as they, over time, work their wills upon innocent features of this planet and reinvent these captive co-inhabitants. How can such strength be beaten down, beaten flat, beaten small?

Paula and Robert's marriage faded similarly. Habits anesthetized passions. Trivialities overcame important moments until the wearing away was the main event, not a catastrophe to fear.

There were moments of possible retrieval.

Paula saw the look her friend gave Robert that first time. She saw Robert brush his fingers against the woman's hip as they sat down to dinner at Paula and Robert's house that night. Robert was quieter at the dinner table, distracted, avoiding their friend's eyes. "Their surrogate sister," they called her. They both loved her like that, had come to trust her and welcome her presence into their home day or night.

Then the persistent forces of nature began the wearing. Clichés explained how their marriage was flattening: the late nights at work, the couple's transformation into strangers, the superficial conversations, hollow but ongoing. But just as predictability marks nature's work, clichés are clichés because of their predictable imposition into life's moments.

Paula had opportunities to stop the erosion. Robert did, too. But they plodded through their daily lives unconsciously, perhaps with hope that what was happening wasn't really happening, perhaps with faith that their early bonds could withstand the washing away, perhaps with resignation that love suffers thus, that their love was still there somewhere, hidden as it was buffeted about. Richie was a testament to their bond, a mutual focus of devotion. Richie was the small tether in their separate revolutions in space.

VII

Robert slept uneasily in the far corner of Paula's hospital room, the shrinking sun slanting through the drawn blinds and lighting up a portion of his face as he slumped in the vinyl armchair. Paula stirred softly in her bed but remained eyes-closed, head still.

Every time you went to her, you broke my heart. Did you know that? You broke my heart.

Her eyes moved sideways beneath her blue-veined eyelids. Her mouth moved slightly. Her neck craned ever-so-imperceptibly toward where Robert slept.

There were many times I wanted to tell you...

She tried to move her hands but couldn't.

I followed you once, from your office. I saw you in her windows. I walked to her door and almost knocked.

Her eyelids flickered, her mouth striving to form speech.

I heard you laughing, her laughing behind that door. I almost knocked. I almost knocked.

The Heavens Weep for Us

Paula's head lay like a stone on the flattened pillow. Her body was small beneath the sheets, small and silent.

But I knew, I knew...

Robert stirred suddenly in the chair, ran a hand across his eyes and nose, shifted positions. His eyes flew open as he looked around the room. He'd been dreaming and had forgotten for the first waking seconds where he was. He looked toward Paula's bed and stared at the quiet form. Suddenly he bolted from his chair and bent over her body. His eyes were wide, alert, and he was holding his breath as he stared at Paula. He stood frozen as he bent closer to her face.

"Paula?" he whispered. He touched her face, her hands. "Paula?"

He placed his fingers on her mouth, her eyes, checking for movement. His hands shook as he checked his wife for any flickerings, shook as he leaned his ear closely to her mouth, checking for words. Had she talked?

Robert straightened up and chuckled softly: "Foolish me."

He stroked her hair automatically, unthinkingly as he stared at her sleeping face.

"At least you're still alive," he said aloud. He gazed at the pale cheeks, the small mouth. This was the woman he'd married a mere ten years ago, a lifetime ago, it seemed. The woman whose spirit he once tucked into his breast, the woman he let go into the rains.

"God, oh God, Paula, please forgive me." He whispered these words as he lay his head on her chest and sobbed.

VIII

"It's been seven months," Dr. Ignacio told Robert.

Robert didn't look up. He was reading some documents from work. He glanced at the calendar he'd pinned near Paula's headboard, then at Paula, who lay quiet and predictable. Then he gazed at his wife's doctor and sighed.

"Yes, that's what it is. Hard to believe, isn't it?" he muttered.

"And how is Richie doing?" asked Dr. Ignacio.

The inference was not lost on Robert. "I brought him here last week. He lay in bed with Paula for a long time." Robert caught his breath at the recollection. "Then he played with her."

"Played with her?"

"He had two of his favorite stuffed toys. He did a whole monologue with them and with his mother." He looked at Paula. "Well, he pretended that his mother was participating. He spoke for her, and the toys, and himself." Robert smiled. "It was a good game."

Dr. Ignacio put his clipboard near Paula's feet and cleared his throat. Robert was back to his paperwork, lost in thought as only he could disappear in the presence of others. Dr. Ignacio knew very well how Robert coped.

"You're here day and night, Robert, sleeping in that lumpy chair..."

Robert chuckled. "Oh, no. I've got a rollaway cot, doc. You just haven't seen it."

"Well, you've hardly seen your kid..."

"I've brought him here many times, doctor. You just haven't been here when Richie's here."

"...hardly see Richie. Your neighbors still caring for him?"

"They're distant relatives and retired from their jobs. Give me a break. Richie's fine, and so am I."

"And you've practically left your job."

"Part-time. I had savings. I work from here." He shuffled some papers for effect.

Dr. Ignacio lowered his gaze. The years of tending to broken people, of hearing broken promises, broken voices, seeing broken spirits lay heavily on him. His face was deeply lined, eyes baggy, but his voice was still firm and clear.

"Just know that it's got to end sometime."

Robert looked up and frowned. "What's got to end?" He thought to himself: *If you'd only seen how it ended.*

"Paula's not coming out of this." The doctor had made his choice. "You've seen the x-rays, the MRI's, EEG's. Her brain cells in a significant portion of her brain were destroyed in that crash."

Robert was incredulous. He'd heard the medical mumbo-jumbo before. How many times? But how could the doctor be giving up? He held his head in his hands as he tried not to listen to Dr. Ignacio.

"Stop fooling yourself!" The doctor leaned down and put his face directly in front of Robert's. Painfully, it reminded Robert of how Paula had sought answers from him that horrible night.

"You've seen all the medical reports, Robert. You—we—can't drag it out anymore. We've got to stop fooling ourselves."

Dr. Ignacio rose and exhaled tiredly. He took a few steps toward Paula, touched the tubes connected to various parts of her, and gazed at the comatose woman.

When Robert spoke, his voice was steady, belying the look on his face. "Can you envision for a moment what her days and nights are like? What if she still *can* hear us and process it and still *feel* pain and frustration because she can't move, can't talk to Richie, to me, to you? She's locked in there somewhere but can't let us know that she's in there!"

The doctor listened but shook his head. "Maybe you feel like your vigil is just beginning. That's what hope does to you. The time doesn't matter anymore. It's a waiting game till hope is proved right."

Robert's frown became more pronounced.

"Robert, we've all seen stories in tabloids about some poor Joe who wakes up after twenty years in a coma. He miraculously returns to his life as if nothing had happened." Dr. Ignacio took a deep breath. "It isn't so. Their brains aren't the same. The more time passes, the worse the prognosis. In Paula's case..." Dr. Ignacio glanced at his patient. "There's nothing there." It hurt him to say this. "Pull the tubes away, and you'll see."

Robert put his papers down and glared at the doctor, glared because anger was easier to deal with than his despair at the doctor's words. He didn't trust his voice anymore. He rose slowly and stood at his wife's bedside. He reached for her hand, swathed it in his, and turned his body away from the doctor. Taking his cue, Dr. Ignacio strode from the room. Outside in the hallway, deserted except for an orderly clearing away trash baskets at the farthest end of the hall, he allowed his façade to fall. He pulled a Kleenex from a box at the end of a nearby counter and wiped his eyes as he headed for the elevator.

He was done for the night.

IX

I can't believe he said those things. He doesn't know

how he's wounded me. He's supposed to be a healer, not a destroyer.

Robert still held his wife's hand. He stroked it rhythmically. He sobbed. He raised her hand to his lips and kissed it tenderly. He stroked her hair and muttered assurances to her, assurances in vain, for he was alone in the room, alone with grief.

Richie played so lovingly. I cherished each word he said, each gibberish. I cherished each little laugh and chuckle. He's so much like you, my angel. I loved how he lay in bed and cuddled.

Robert sat on the edge of Paula's bed. He leaned over to kiss her warm, unlined forehead.

You've made great sacrifices for me, my darling. No matter what happens, I'll never forget how you've stood by me. I never want you to leave.

He closed his eyes as he invoked scenes from happier times, from before the coma. He smiled at the memories.

You have no idea how much I love you. If I never told you enough times before the accident, please hear me now. Despite the lost times, despite all that. Please hear me! I love you, Robert.

With an exclamation, Robert stood suddenly. He leaned close to his wife's silent face. Gasping, with his fingers quivering, he touched her cheeks and wiped the glistening wetness away.

Faithless

Wash him off now. Whatever his name was, I'm washing him away. Never brings them here. No, this is her home, her and her husband's, to be honored.

Faithless

S
he really loves her husband, but here she is. The face that replaces absence, the surrogate arms. She doesn't remember his name, but he's quietly intent on understanding hers.

"So your name's Sandy?"

She gazes at him with immobile eyes, inscrutable mouth. For the third time, she tells him: "It's not Sandy. It's Faith." She doesn't understand why she cares that he get her name right. His was a wisp of air as soon as he rolled over on his back the first time last night and began modulating his breath.

"I don't get it," he replies. "It's Santa, ain't it? I wouldn't want to be called that. Sandy's a natural."

"I'm not a Sandy," she says quietly. She doesn't smoke, doesn't drink, so, after copulating, she never has the convenience of those little acts that strangers engage in, busily or lazily, to pass the minutes that now don't count anyway. Minutes between minutes, at best. Still, he is here now, and her husband isn't, so she slides into her role again and props herself up on her elbow.

Smoothly now, she says: "My name is Santa Fe Santana. If you really want an English translation, it's *Holy Faith Saint Ann.* That's me. I'm not a Sandy. I'm not a Santa. I'm Faith." She shrugs her slender shoulders and summons up some sweetness as she pecks his cheek. Strange-man stubble bristles on her chin.

He laughs suddenly. She finds her immobile eyes and mouth again, steadies her gaze once more, loses the ersatz sweetness. "What?"

He drawls: "Your mama, or whoever named you, sure had a high-falutin' image of you for the future, huh?" He laughs again, inhales deeply on his cigarette, and adds: "Saint? Huh! Faith? Huh and double huh!" Now he props himself on an elbow, stubbly smile vibrating slightly in the corner, and peers into her somber face.

"Ain't you married?"

His laughter shakes the early morning darkness as it jostles her tremulous dignity.

For four years, actually. Faith has been married for four years. She turns the key in her door, lets herself in, goes straight to her bathroom. Wash him off now. Whatever his

70

name was, I'm washing him away. She has the ritual down pat. Never brings them here. No, this is her home, her and her husband's, to be honored. She goes to men and never for more than one night with any of them. Never.

Her shroud of privacy is lifted only once each time, only once, when she tells them her name. It's Faith. For a reason she has been unable to grasp these past two years, laying open her identity to strange men whose strange homes she has just entered has never bothered her. The men's identities are proverbial water, sliding past the fingers of her consciousness as soon as their fingers begin touching her. She lays open her body to them, so why is her name any more important?

She scrubs her belly and thighs hard, the water as hot as she can endure. Washing him away, she thinks, her eyes crinkling in the shower stream, water mixing with water. Washing him away. She has the ritual down pat.

She dreams. The ivory sheers at her open window flutter slowly, seemingly in rhythm with her breathing. In her bed, her soul battles through the night. She floats through the grayness and debris of her dreams surrounded by smoke, tinged with unease. Disembodied among dervish sands, she always seeks him, sometimes glimpses him beyond ruined houses. Men and women in robes, children without legs scream in words she can't decipher. Storms, shouts, rattling sounds entwirl girls running among rocks, stones. Some dreams she recalls upon awakening. But always there is the moistness on her face, the nightgown clinging to her limbs, the rapid breath.

Thus she heralds daylight.

Breakfast is quick, always immemorable, just an obligatory stop on her way to the computer. She tackles her email with every cell of her body on alert, blood coursing, eyes alive. She scrolls down the screen directly to her husband's name. Yes, oh God yes, there it is! She mutters softly as her fingers stroke her computer screen. She touches her hands palm to palm, shuts her eyes softly, before opening his message to her.

Politics mean nothing to Faith. The president blends into the background of her television set, gray, dark blue, white, indecipherable, indistinguishable. His men at the microphone with him, or striding toward the helicopter, reporters in tow, look alike, their talk equally vacuous. They're all alike. All the men. They do what they want in this world, care what they care, get what they want, and everyone else is a blob of nothingness to them that fades and runs together, just as they're a monstrous nothing to Faith. She tries not to dwell on this.

She was barely nineteen when she married Luke, but

she already knew what it's all about. "Age doesn't dictate wisdom," she said when her parents disapproved. "Age doesn't dictate wisdom," she said again to Luke's parents a few days later. "I've been around the block," she joked, but her heart had thrashed inside her ribs at the thought that he wouldn't be the one, after all, for her. She knew he was, but the roadblocks parents throw into their children's paths often bely their love.

Faith prevailed, but she and Luke were married scarcely two years when he was called away, not by official dictum but by his own sense of what men do in times like these. Nothing kept him at her side. Not love burning brighter than their ignited wisdom. Nothing.

Nothing, she thinks, staring at his photo on her bedside table. Her quilts cannot muffle her regret.

How many? she wonders. In the end, does it matter? Headlines assault her, as the deaths spread across two nations, as solicitous co-workers coddle her with unstated fears, as television drivel merges deception with death. Each day she lives with only the certainty of uncertainty. Luke's sporadic email messages to her hold no keys to knowing, really knowing. His distant, dusty land holds hurt, not hope.

As she bucks and groans in another man's bed, everything coalesces and seems fleetingly clear. Sameness is the everlasting current. Longings flail against a curtain that rose momentarily to throw you a glimpse of possibilities, then smothered itself shut. Better to step away, to remember that nothing keeps.

KeiKei & Ollie

This is as it should be, Amy thought to herself. Him on that side, me on this side. Each of us in our respective places, each of us where we belong.

KeiKei & Ollie

"Quite a love story," murmured Amy, as she gazed at KeiKei and Ollie curled up together on her bedroom carpet.

KeiKei, the young Siamese cat, stretched and looked up at Amy, as if she'd understood, then pushed her silky body closer to Ollie, the black and white Australian shepherd snoring away. Ollie was almost twelve now, and his thick fur was striated with white hairs where black had dominated not long ago. The two animals were quite a pair as they lay in the semi-darkness, with KeiKei almost a perfect little circle between Ollie's large, outstretched legs.

Amy tiptoed around them as she finished putting her laundry away and tidying up the room. Unfortunately, this is what weekends were for. Living alone, never married, childless, thirty-something Amy looked forward to Saturday so she could catch up with the rest of her life, the non-job-related one. She grunted and shook her head at the thought of this.

Amazing! she chuckled. *What a life.*

Distracting herself, she gazed at her two companions as they slept. They'd started out as across-the-street neighbors, these two. Amy's jovial, Harley-driving, tattooed, gentle-bear neighbor had six other cats besides KeiKei, so when his youngest feline became a regular fixture at Amy's house, her neighbor really didn't mind. KeiKei had met Ollie at her house on one of Amy's visits across the street two years ago and had immediately taken a liking to the ten-year-old, mellowed Ollie. The other cats, in various stages of disinterest and arrogance, had either hidden quickly or had tried to stare down the dog, eventually going about their personal business and not caring one way or the other. But KeiKei had been remarkable, small cat that she was, in coming right up to Ollie, sniffing him down, and deciding on the spot that he was something special. KeiKei followed him and Amy home that day, then started paying house calls on a somewhat regular basis.

Amy went into the bathroom. She brushed her dark hair into a smooth ponytail, refreshed her lipstick, and changed into a fresh shirt. She looked at the clock. Right on target, KeiKei swished into the small room and rubbed against Amy. Then slowly, on tiptoes so as not to awaken Ollie, she let herself out the open side door. This was KeiKei's routine: come over, spend the day with Ollie, then, just before dinnertime—remembering who her lord and master really was—sashay across the street to finish out her languorous day.

As Ollie slept, Amy locked her front door and ran her Saturday afternoon errands. First to the post office, where, as usual, there was nothing special in her PO box. Then to the dry cleaner's, where she picked up her coming week's wardrobe and chatted for a few minutes with the brother-sister owners of the shop, delightful young Armenians who had a gift for remembering every patron's name and something about their lives.

"So how are the two lovebirds?" the girl asked Amy, chuckling.

Amy described how Ollie and KeiKei were getting closer all the time.

"I tell you. They're the classic odd couple," said Amy. "Frankly, I don't know what they see in each other."

The three laughed at that and exchanged a few more pleasantries. Amy complimented the brother on his new haircut and hurried out to her last stop of the evening: her favorite take-out eatery, The Four Corners. She'd been a regular patron there for almost three years now, since the restaurant had opened, but she never quite felt fully at home there and also didn't quite know why.

Well, maybe she had an inkling.

As she walked up to the front door, she knew she had to face him.

He belonged to a different era. Long, long ago, his ancestors had walked upon different earth, dust of centuries, stones of millennia past. Had walked under skies thousands of miles away, under stars that decorated nights, then burnt themselves into oblivion. That land was his land, and his father's, and *his* father's, for how long into the past? But this little corner of California was his land now, with multilingual signs lining both sides of the crowded city street, neon lights competing for attention, tiny booths of vendors squeezed snugly among the 99¢ Store, Rite-Aid Pharmacy, Mexican restaurants, Chinese fast-foods, and other odds and ends of enterprise that collided and co-existed in this particular corner of the four corners of the world.

His swarthy skin glistened with a fine veneer of sweat. Sweat beaded like clear tiny pearls around his upper lip. His small beard wrapped around his square chin and connected with his close-cropped sideburns and short black hair. His eyebrows were thick, almost meeting one another at the top of his long, sleek nose. When he smiled, which was rarely, his teeth were small and yellowish but perfectly shaped. She saw him minutes before he noticed her, and she quietly observed him as he spoke briefly to customers, walking briskly from table to table, then sliding behind the counter to ring up sales with a calm, focused expression on his face. He embodied these two opposites—energetic activity and serenity—and moved between the two quietly, smoothly. This was, after all, his restaurant, his livelihood, the most important thing he owned in this world.

Amy waited by the tall potted ficus near the entrance, not wanting to imply any sense of hurried imposition by standing at the counter. Soon, Joe, as he called himself, saw her and immediately brightened. He reached under the counter for a fresh, starched towel, draped it over his forearm, and came forward to kiss her hand. He bowed slightly and swept his toweled arm out in a gentle arc.

"Now the sun is really shining in here," he said in his soft, heavily accented voice.

Amy flushed, as always. After all these months of hearing such compliments from Joe, it was still uncomfortable to her, although—she had to admit this—part of her liked his attention. She sometimes had trouble meeting his eyes, since his were intense and focused in an examining way when he looked at her. He wasn't that way with everyone else, she'd noted a long time ago. So she looked briefly at him now, averted her gaze, and spoke as calmly as her discomfort allowed her. Joe was older than she, older, calmer, and patient. He waited for her to respond.

"You probably say that to everyone, Joe." She knew he

didn't, but it was all she could muster to parry his flattery. She felt trite. Joe, for his part, sensed this and chose not to answer. He swept his arm toward a small, marble-topped table in a bay window toward the back of his restaurant. It was a table for two, private, sitting coolly under tall, hanging fronds from two enormous potted palms at either end of the window.

"Oh, no. Not necessary," she stammered. "Actually, I'm just taking food to go." They looked at one another, and she chuckled. "Again. I guess I'm just a to-go type of person!"

He knew she wasn't. She wasn't someone passing through, which is what he thought of when he heard "to go." No, she was someone that should stay. She was someone he wanted to sit forever in his restaurant so he could see her face, her eyes, her hair, and enjoy his work even more, seeing the sunshine she carried with her all the time. At least all the times he saw her at The Four Corners, for that was the only place he ever saw Amy. Though he wished that were different.

"No, no," he countered. "Stay." Still bowing slightly, he pulled out a brown wrought iron chair at the table, held it for her, his heart thumping. For the first time, Amy felt that Joe wasn't in control. She sensed vulnerability. Their eyes met, his soulful, hers unsure. But it was his gaze that flickered. The pearls of sweat on his lip shimmied ever so slightly as his gaze locked on hers. For a fleeting second, she felt lost, but as he seemed weaker, she felt stronger. Some of her discomfort faded.

"No, I'm taking a plate to go," she said in a low voice. She was able to continue looking at his face as she spoke. She noticed for the first time that he had a scar on his left cheek that was almost hidden by his beard, and she wondered briefly how he'd gotten the scar, and if the beard was meant as a camouflage. Finally, Joe lowered his gaze, put the chair back, and walked hurriedly to the counter to take her order.

Amy felt flustered, though her exterior was cool. *This is as it should be*, Amy thought to herself. *Him on that side, me on this side. Each of us in our respective places, each of us where we belong. How can it be otherwise?* She gathered the wrapped package, thanked him, and finished her thought:

"*...and never the twain shall meet.*"

Ollie was awake when Amy returned home. He was curious about the package she held, sniffing it energetically. But she was hungry, and tonight she didn't share her dinner.

KeiKei roused Amy the next day. Amy had forgotten to close the side door fully, tired as she was from staying up late finishing work from her job. KeiKei entered the darkened bedroom and went straight to Amy's face, licking her cheeks and kneading her shoulders. KeiKei didn't wait for a response but went in short order to Ollie's corner of the room and cuddled instantly with the big dog. Ollie was lethargic, still sleepy obviously, but he responded willingly to the little cat's maneuverings and allowed KeiKei to curl up between his paws. The two settled in for some extra snooze time as Amy groaned in bed and decided she might as well get up.

As she dressed by her closet's sliding door, Amy gazed at the dog and cat. Old and young. Big and little. Serene and spunky. Stay-at-home and range-the-wide-field. Scruffy and lumbering versus elegant and lithe. She remembered briefly her college years, when she herself had been young and spunky, and—she liked to think of it this way—lithe and elegant. Not that it had gotten her anywhere, romance-wise. Though Amy had graduated magna cum laude from one of the finest California universities, one of the top in the world, actually, Amy had certainly not achieved in the man-snagging arena. Her glistening, silky hair, expressive brown eyes, and well-toned figure had caught the attention of plenty of so-called eligible bachelors, and she'd had her share of dates in well-appointed places with well-heeled suitors. She'd thrived in her arena of homogeneity, actually, her circle of social class sameness, of elite high achievers sipping coffee at the trendiest coffeehouses, taking the right exotic cruises, studying with the best professor advisors. Sameness was good for her, had rescued her from worrying about not fitting in, coming as she did from a dusty little Texas town. Yes, sameness had been good to her.

In her thirties now, Amy had the career, the portfolio, the cozy but all-paid-for townhouse in an iconic, dynamic community—everything she'd aimed for. But she was alone. Not counting KeiKei and Ollie, of course, Amy was alone. Somewhere along the way, she'd grown up in her own skin, had tossed on her shoulders the mantle of her own identity, the "Texan Californian done good." She began drifting away from sameness and realized she could still thrive when everything and everyone around her didn't fit neatly like cooperative puzzle pieces in an easy Brookstone puzzle board. Somewhere along the way, also, Amy had slipped into her singleness with the same amount of resistance she'd use in easing into a comfy pair of slippers. The years and her aloneness coursed by hand in hand, on parallel tracks, so that being alone became inseparable from growing older.

She gazed at her reflection in a hallway mirror. Some crow's feet, though very fine at this stage. *OK*, she thought, *not so bad.* She tossed her hair back, admiring the way the morning sun glinted off her mane. Not bad. She still had it. She still *had game!* But what men were milling about?

Who was phoning her? Who was hot for her? Not a soul. She sat at the foot of her bed to tie the sandal straps around her ankles. She wondered fleetingly if her career was sucking out any chances of romance in her life.

Well, there is somebody, she thought. She paused and brought his face to her mind's eye. Joe flirted with her, though she'd hardly call it flirting in the old sense of the word. *His eyes speak volumes,* she thought. He didn't treat other women as he treated her, or at least not when Amy was there in the restaurant. He was exotic, had a certain handsomeness to him, a certain vibrance and maturity, a seriousness that many men her age today lacked. As she got to know Joe better, her heart sometimes played tiny tricks on her, like beating a little bit faster. She was having a bit more trouble facing his intense gaze.

Smoldering, she thought. *His smoldering gaze.*

Yes, she knew he was interested in her. She recalled briefly a recent day when she had tied Ollie outside the restaurant, and Joe had calmed the dog while she went inside and ordered. She smiled as she remembered Joe squatting on the pavement, his apron still on, his face calm as he stroked the dog.

Kindred spirits connecting on the sidewalk, she told herself. Mellow, wise, gray hair among black. Reliable, gentle, strong. She surprised herself with these descriptions before reality sank in. The reality of old. The pull of sameness had not totally dissipated. Joe was from a different realm, an alien world, as attractive as he might seem to her at times. Amy with Joe? No way.

Ollie and KeiKei, now stirring for their morning sunbath upstairs on the deck, stretched and gave Amy a few consoling leg rubs. They sashayed out the side door and left her wondering if she minded anymore. If she minded being alone. Being older and alone.

She really wasn't sure.

The Four Corners of the World. That was the full name of Joe's restaurant when he and his family—mother, father, younger brother—had first opened their doors in Silver Lake. But then, just like Federal Express became FedEx, and Kentucky Fried Chicken became KFC, and California Federal Bank became CalFed, and on and on with downsized names, Joe, then his family, decided that they needed to be, instead, The Four Corners.

"People will still make the connection. We're the 'corners of the world,'" Joe had explained. "Who knows?" he'd added jokingly. "Maybe someday we'll be so famous, we can just be called 'The 4C.'" He'd written the abbreviated name on a napkin. They all laughed together.

"JLo and KFed, move over!" the younger Polo had exclaimed.

Eleven years younger than Joe, Polo was the most

Americanized in the family. Sometimes this rubbed the family wrong. Sometimes they were proud of him for fitting in so well in their adopted land.

And sometimes they felt their adopted land didn't return the sentiment. It was not easy, though among immigrants, certainly their lot was better than that of many. They had come to this land with a solid education and some money. They were independent businesspeople, which enabled them to control their moneymaking better than those who worked for others. For the most part, each day was comprised of hard work, long hours, striving to make customers happy, doing what small businesses had to do to survive. That left little time for laughter among Joe's family. Little time for fun, for making friends, for…romance.

As he thanked the last customer of the evening and began wiping down tables, Joe was suddenly alone with his thoughts. This was the time, the time when he could allow himself to acknowledge what he felt, what he thought, what he desired. At these hours, his father would clean the back area, with his mother preparing items for the next business day. Polo would be unloading boxes and organizing supplies. So Joe, the front man, the heart and soul of The Four Corners, though no one in the family or anywhere else ever stated this, was at the front of the store, blinds closed, the "Open" sign flipped over, lights mostly out except for whatever lighting was needed for him to tidy up the front, to close out the cash register for the day, to prepare The 4C for tomorrow. It was at this late hour of the night, only at these late hours, when Joe thought about Joe, wondered about Joe, speculated about Joe's path in life, and wished happy things for Joe.

Like Amy.

She did indeed bring sunshine in with her whenever she entered his restaurant. The first time he saw her, she'd stepped briskly to the counter, long hair loose on either side of her shoulders, a yellow sundress showing off her bronzed skin. But it was the expression on her face—serious, serene, alert, kind—that had caught his attention fully. Though she was not smiling when she spoke to him, ordering #6 on the takeout menu, please, something about her demeanor made him feel that she *was* smiling, that she was smiling directly at him, and only at him. Her small mouth was relaxed, her eyes soft, though her voice was the voice of a woman who was probably used to being in charge. In retrospect now, as he wiped down the last group of tables for the night, Joe was astounded at himself for having seen so much, having understood so much about Amy in those first few minutes of seeing her. For, as time proved, he'd been right about her, about the woman who carried sunshine that first day and every day thereafter.

"*A single sunbeam is enough to drive away many shadows*,'" Joe muttered to himself, smiling in the gloom of the restaurant. He looked awkwardly behind him, toward the back room where his family was, hoping that no one had heard him. He stopped wiping for a moment, savored the sentiment by St. Francis of Assisi that Joe had learned in the old country, in his English class, long before he ever came to America. He shook his head gently and smiled to himself.

This American woman, this Amy, was an enigma. She was one of his most regular customers, sometimes sitting in the bay window and lingering over her meal while she worked on papers, no doubt *important* papers, thought Joe. Lost in thought, she'd sometimes take her brown hair, twirl it around into a tight snake, as long-haired women are so adept at doing, and prop it in place with a pencil, or something miraculous like that. She could sit lost in thought and work for an entire afternoon, sporadically ordering a new cup of tea to keep her going. She would say little, interact not at all, yet still radiate the serenity and kindness Joe had noticed from the start. Joe marveled at her.

At other times, Amy would dash in with her briefcase held out at an angle at her side, to keep from banging against it in her hurry, and order to go. When she came in during the week, especially before five o'clock, she was dressed in dark, elegant clothes befitting the important papers she no doubt carried in that briefcase. When she came in during the weekends, her hair was often loose, clothing relaxed, pace dramatically slowed. It was at these times, the weekend times, when Joe felt he could understand her, when he had golden moments here and there of making small talk, of getting to know this woman who had captivated him.

I feel her heart. I see her heart. I can almost touch her heart, Joe thought as he worked. *And that beautiful heart should be mine.* He looked awkwardly behind him again, as if his thoughts were audible.

She already has my heart, he thought. Then sadly: *How can she not know?*

Then: *Or not care?*

Recently, on a Saturday morning, Amy had come to The Four Corners with her dog, a large, hairy creature with big, black spots streaked with gray and a bushy tail. She called the dog Ollie. She had tied it to a parking meter outside the restaurant, but the dog had cried and struggled against its leash when Amy had tried to walk away. Joe had witnessed this and dashed outside to assist. Amy was surprised. Joe calmed the dog, distracted it by stroking its long fur, and Ollie had slowly settled into the pavement, stretched his paws, and leisurely licked Joe's hand. Joe said to Amy, "You go on in. Polo will take your order."

Amy had stood still for a moment. She looked at Ollie, looked at Joe. Then she stared at Joe, as much to say, "Wow. You know, you don't have to do this." Joe looked calmly up at her, still stroking Ollie, who now lay serenely on the shaded pavement and blissfully licked Joe's other hand. Amy ducked inside.

When she came out, drink and bag in hand, she bestowed a torrent of sunshine upon Joe.

She leaned over, kissed him lightly on his cheek, smiled hugely at him, and took Ollie home.

Ollie and KeiKei were married. Or, at least, they should be. They should have been wedded on live TV, so that humans could learn how to love and how to live in love. This is what Amy felt about her two companions, her dear friends, but she realized how ridiculous it all sounded, especially coming from a career woman who prided herself on her intelligence, her rationality, her sophistication. She doted on this dog and cat and oftentimes chuckled when she remembered the iconic line from Dan Akroyd's comedy, "Ghostbusters," regarding the appalling idea of "dogs and cats living together."

KeiKei and Ollie were inseparable. Whether they sunbathed side by side, ate their meals in tandem, trotted alongside Amy on their respective leashes when she took walks around her neighborhood, or merely snoozed by the TV set when Amy kicked back with her remote control in hand, the two furries were a testament to togetherness. When they slept, curled into one another, Amy oftentimes took great pleasure watching them, just sitting near them and watching them as they melded into one body of fur without boundaries.

The lesson was not lost on Amy. She, once the worshipper of Sameness, the devotee of sticking-with-your-own-kind through her college years and beyond, she—the Texan Californian who should have known better—felt her being stretch itself, stretch into new understandings, new sympathies as the months and years passed, and KeiKei and Ollie grew alongside her: the old, the young, and the lonely.

In Southern California, the seasons roll into one another with little distinction among them. Summer heat dissipates and turns things of nature over to Indian summers in the fall, which knock leaves off trees, cool the evening air a tad more, and prepare to turn over the keys to winter. Winter drags its feet, throwing in some chilly days and nights and sporadic rains, never having the heart to obliterate the perennial greenery and sunshine of this particular corner of earth. So the months merge one into the other, and time passes faster than Californians know.

And so it was that the third year of Joe and Amy knowing one another came to a close without fanfare. But Joe told himself on a lonely, dusky night of wiping tables that the time was long past for him to reach out for her heart.

He had to still his, to make his feelings known. Today would be the day. Moving quickly, before fear could freeze his intentions, Joe committed himself to…what did the Americans call it?

"Sticking my neck out," he murmured to himself as he drove to work in the early morning darkness. The phrase somewhat frightened him, as it evoked decapitation. But he was committed.

At The Four Corners, he asked his mother to prepare a queenly dish for the evening, something not on the menu. She was immediately curious, but she did not want to cast any bad luck on whatever plan her elder son was brewing. He was, after all, the reason for the success of The 4C, as the family good-naturedly, secretly had begun calling their restaurant. His good business sense, his genuine way with the people, and his determination to follow his head had brought much good luck to their restaurant. He had brought his family—father, mother, brother—to Silver Lake and had tutored them in the ways of America. She began gathering the necessary ingredients for the special dish as soon as she put her apron on first thing in the morning.

Polo's task this day was to cover for Joe whenever Joe had to leave the register. Joe, for his part, rearranged some of the large, potted plants, which had grown remarkably well in the past few years, to create a deep bower, more lush, more intimate, despite its spot at the front bay window. Though all the tables in The 4C were now topped with thick, sparkling glass over henna-colored tablecloths, Joe placed a stiffly-starched white tablecloth on the small table in the bay window. He went, during a brief break before lunchtime, to a florist around the corner and bought a small crystal vase with three yellow roses and baby's breath. He gently placed this in the center of the table for two and set a hand-printed sign beside the vase: "RESERVED." Not knowing if Amy would come into his restaurant at lunchtime or dinnertime, he had to move fast. Either way, he sighed, he was ready for her arrival.

And arrive she did.

Without her sunshine.

But with dark glasses on. Large, black-rimmed glasses that covered half her face. The restaurant closed at ten, and she shuffled in at nine. Joe was behind the counter, arranging the menus, repressing his disappointment in her failure to show. When he looked up, he caught his breath. At long last, she was here, but something was wrong.

He responded instinctively and without his usual flourishes.

"Shadows follow you today, Amy. My heart feels sad to see your sadness."

He waited quietly, but Amy was silent, unmoving. After several moments, her mouth quivered subtly. He came around the counter and gently held her elbow. He led her to the most quiet, private place in his restaurant: the bower, though the plan was now changed. But Amy needed privacy. He pulled out a chair for her, and she noticed the "RESERVED" sign as he did so.

"Oh, I can't sit here," she began. "You need this...."

"Sshh. Sshh," he hushed her softly, guiding her to sit, gently pushing in the chair. "This table is for you." He felt a bit foolish saying it now, since the scene was nothing like he'd imagined. She looked up quickly at him and wanted to speak but remained wordless. He motioned to Polo to take over at the counter, as per their agreement, and folded his arms on the table as he looked at Amy. Moments passed, and she remained still, unspeaking. Her head was bowed, and Joe could see that she intended to say something and was merely waiting for the strength to talk. He was patient. He motioned for Polo to bring a pot of hot tea to the table.

Amy removed her glasses, and Joe understood why she'd hidden her face. Her eyes were swollen, almost swollen shut, the eyes of a woman who has wept too much, too long. Her cheeks were red, glossy, and even now tears waited in the creases of her eyelids, ready to flow again. What could be wrong?

"Ollie is dying." She whispered the words quickly, so fast and soft that Joe almost didn't catch them. Joe had never seen her sad, could not have imagined how sad and devastated her face could look. "I had to get away. I couldn't bear to watch him anymore." She seemed ashamed she'd left him at home in his despair.

Joe's command of English, imperfect as it was, abandoned him quickly. He was stunned. He fished in his mind for words to say.

"I know you cared about Ollie," Amy continued. She recalled the time Joe stayed outside the restaurant with Ollie. He remembered it clearly. Amy folded her arms on the table and sank her head into them. She started weeping. Joe brought his chair around beside hers and gently placed his hand on her shoulder. He fought the urge to wrap his arm around her.

"Ollie's my best friend," she said. She didn't care if she sounded childish. She was now in the presence of this unusual man who seemed to understand her, to know her heart, who'd cared about her all this time without saying so. She straightened up and wiped her face with both hands. Joe quickly grabbed a clean napkin from an adjoining table and handed it to her. He sat back down beside her, a bit closer, and kept his left hand lightly, respectfully on her shoulder.

Amy wiped her cheeks, looking at Joe all the time she did so. Joe watched her calmly, patiently. All the compassion possible in a human being was in the dark pools of his gaze. Amy let herself slip into those dusky, cooling pools and absorb their healing. She slowly reached for his other hand on the table and covered it with hers. She leaned her head on his shoulder. At this, Joe let his left hand slide gently across her back to rest on her other shoulder. He sighed deeply, audibly as he allowed her to rest against him and to continue weeping.

"Will you come with me?" she asked. "Will you help me with Ollie?"

He wept, too. The waiting and wondering of three years flowed steadily away from him, and his tears of commiseration now were also tears of gratitude and hope.

Fooled

But the forces of conspiracy whispered in the kitchen, in the basement, outside under the mesquite tree. Too weak. No, no. Can't tell her. Have to keep fooling her. Have to.

Fooled

They didn't tell her that her daughter was dead. They figured it was best that she not know.

Just like they didn't tell her that her brother Samuel had died almost one year ago of a heart attack. And, before him by ten months, her youngest brother Aldo of pneumonia. Her heart wouldn't be able to take it, they said. Too weak. She's too old. Shouldn't know.

So Magdalena didn't know about the car accident in New Mexico, didn't know about Cora lying in the faraway hospital for three weeks before succumbing to her injuries. Didn't know about the funeral in Albuquerque, the hundreds of people who'd known Cora who were discreetly shushed away by the family, all in the interest of keeping the death and burial as quiet as they could.

It was easy to do this. Magdalena—"Maggie," they all called the old woman—was sequestered enough. Feeble enough. With kidneys failing, eyesight almost a mere memory, widowhood, and four years of social reclusiveness bolstered by the beginnings of Alzheimer's, Maggie was easy to fool. That's what they said, crossing themselves as they whispered in rooms farthest from hers, in the only house she'd ever owned, her children's childhood home. Thank God she was so easy to fool.

So when she asked about Samuel or Aldo, as she always asked about relatives who hadn't distinguished themselves by solicitousness toward her or by frequent visits to her bedside, her family was evasive...or downright dishonest.

"I'm not sure. Haven't heard from him in a while now." Or, "Well, when I saw him recently, he looked great."

Then they scrambled to distract her, change the topic suavely. After all, Maggie came from a large family, and there were plenty of other relatives to inquire about. And so the family chattered amongst themselves about all the live ones, who went where, did what, and said whatever. Maggie easily embroiled herself in chit-chat about all these folks, many of whom she hadn't seen in years or spoken to in decades. Family was always a viable topic of conversation with her. Minor dementia aside, her recollections of events long shrouded in forgetfulness for everyone else were sometimes quite stunning to her family.

"Remember when I got sick on my honeymoon? The

Acapulco doctors didn't know how to keep me down," she'd giggle. Or, "Your father's parents died of the flu in 1918, remember? They didn't leave a penny of inheritance to any of their kids. That's why your father never went back to school."

Sometimes Maggie wept at mention of her husband, whom she'd loved unfailingly for fifty-one years until his departure from their world of an illness no doctors could name if they'd wanted to. It wouldn't have mattered to Maggie anyway. What killed her husband paled by what sucked her spirit out so swiftly. These things didn't need names, only antidotes.

Her days for years had been indistinguishable one from the other. Her bones, tissue-paper skeleton, began betraying her before her kidneys had, before her eyes abandoned her in the mistaken notion that they weren't needed anymore. She'd stopped reading a few months after her husband died, stopped going to church after she fell one Christmas Eve on the slippery wooden steps moistened with dew. Her doctor came to her, like the proverbial mountain dominated by Mohammed, so even the medical office visitations that had filled a vacuum became, in short order, anachronistic inconveniences for Maggie.

"Why hasn't Cora phoned me?" she asked one day. Silence. "It's been too long," she continued. "It isn't like her to forget about me." She looked from one face to the other.

One left the room quickly, taking the leftover lunch and dirty dishes from the bedside table. The other brought his chair closer to Maggie's bed in preparation for creativity.

"Oh, she called the other day, Ma, but you were sleeping, and I didn't want to wake you."

She peered closely at him. Surprising himself, he shifted in his chair slightly and cleared his throat. Minutes passed, and Maggie said nothing. Only stared. Stared and glanced down at her hands, then peered at him again.

"You know how important her calls are to me." He did know, so he shifted again and fished in his mind for something that might placate her. "You should have awakened me."

"You were sleeping so soundly, Ma. You'd had a rough night. You needed your rest."

Maggie didn't seem convinced.

"Get Cora on the phone now," she said simply.

He looked at the clock on the wall, checked his wristwatch. "Oh, she's still at work right now. You know how she's never at her desk anyway. She walks all over that place, usually forgets her cell phone. Remember? Best not to disturb her now, Ma."

Maggie looked crushed.

"I'll call her when she gets out," he said confidently. "Don't worry about her."

She closed her eyes, pulled the blanket closer to her

chin, and exhaled long and longingly. She wanted to talk to Cora. Her baby. Her youngest child, the brightest star in her constellation of angels. Of her five children, Cora had always been the frontrunner for her unmitigated affection. Child of light. Child of evanescent joy.

Child conceived in an exquisite, moonlit balcony high above a Florida beach on a vacation long, long ago. Child of passion ratcheted up to an unbelievable level, not to be outdone by gods themselves. Child to seal our bond to one another, her husband had said upon Cora's entrance to the world.

She wanted to speak to her beloved Cora.

But the forces of conspiracy whispered in the kitchen, in the basement, outside under the mesquite tree. Too weak. No, no. Can't tell her. Have to keep fooling her. Have to.

And so it went.

"I got her on the phone after work," he said to her later. "I looked in on you, and you were fast asleep."

"Why didn't you wake me?"

"Oh, but I did. You mumbled in your sleep. I shook your shoulder, but you were zonked out, Ma. I couldn't get you to wake up."

Maggie looked at him as if seeing him for the first time. A stranger. A stranger in her home, was it? She said nothing.

And so it went. She asked for Samuel and Aldo a few more times, each mention of these dead ones growing farther apart. They were always out of town, or sleeping when her family called them, or in the shower or restroom. The conspiracy was so carefully orchestrated, that all of them knew what to say and how to say it. Cousins, aunts, uncles. They were all in on the fooling. After all, it was for the best.

Her queries about Cora died a harder death. She'd sometimes preface her request to speak to her youngest child with an anecdote, an impossibly endearing story of something Cora had done, or had said, when she was a little girl. Then they would all laugh at the recollection, add more details, like a rondelle, smile at one another with their remembrances of the pig-tailed ball of energy they all knew was their mother's favorite. They'd share story after story of how Cora had won the school's spelling bee, or had broken her arm when she'd fallen out of a tree while waiting for the ice cream truck, or had fallen asleep on the school bus after the Winter Field Trip and had been the last one dropped off. They all doted on Cora.

But Maggie received no calls from her. Her dementia wasn't this advanced yet. It couldn't be possible that Maggie was indeed speaking with Cora and not remembering. No, the rush of warmth at hearing her daughter's voice could not be dismissed. She either felt it or she didn't. She either spoke with Cora or she didn't. There was no confusion about this. There was no way she'd be wrong on this.

Maggie looked at her son, his wife, her other sons and all the other people—sometimes unrecognizable to her—who rotated in and out of her house to care for her, to feed her, to clean and clothe her, to read to her, to pray with her. She watched their bustling, heard the dishes rattling in the sink as they washed them. She watched them tiptoeing around her room when they thought she was asleep. Their ministering to her was selfless, a product of their love for her, worthless, weak old woman that she was. This she felt. This she called herself. But she understood her family's devotion and accepted how things were.

For weeks they continued the charade. For weeks Maggie ate her meals—or pretended to eat her meals—in her darkened bedroom. She chatted sporadically with them for entertainment, no longer just about family. Maggie watched television sometimes, napped more frequently, snapped at her visiting doctor more frequently. Sometimes Maggie refused her pills. Sometimes Maggie pretended to take the pills but didn't. When they turned their backs momentarily—to get her the pillow at the foot of her bed, perhaps, or to get an extra blanket she requested—Maggie sometimes dropped her pills behind the nightstand. They didn't know the old woman was doing this.

And so it went. It was best this way. Weak. Hearts

couldn't take it.

When the day came for Maggie's invalidity to meet its end, she glanced at them all through foggy, blurry eyes. Her family stood bravely around her bed, hands clasped in front of them, some weeping softly, others fighting to stem their tears. She wanted to speak to them, to tell them she knew, to tell them she understood.

Voiceless, she smiled momentarily, closed her eyes, and sighed when she recognized the three she knew would come, especially her child of light. The ones who'd been waiting for her throughout the fooling, waiting in the wings of heaven.

Victim

The policeman stood a few feet from her window and aimed his flashlight beam on her face. She blinked again, turned away, and felt that she'd cry if he hassled her the slightest bit.

Victim

She ran across the dimly-lit street, dodging cars that honked at her irascibly for not using the crosswalk ten yards away. She ran on tiptoes, almost carelessly, a lithe figure impaled occasionally in angry headlights. She was breathless as she reached her car in the dark parking lot across the campus, as she dug into her purse for the keys. She turned her body to allow as much light as possible from the lamp post a quarter block off to strike her purse.

"Damn!" she muttered, still digging. Her fingernail caught in the groove of her keyring, and she jerked her hand out of her purse, tears already forming because she knew her nail was broken. She sucked it, muttering once again while tears flowed. "Oh damn. Oh damn." She nursed her stub of a nail, its jagged outline a dim, incongruous juxtaposition to four beautifully-tapering ovals. What a night! The thought struck her that she should be glad she hadn't been waylaid there alone in the darkness, as she'd fumbled stupidly for her keys.

She drove quickly away, her car jerking, almost stalling as she rounded the corner. It was a dark street, as, ironically, most university streets were. Authorities marveled at the high incidence of assaults on such a prestigious campus, a campus almost in the heart of town and not more than three miles from the closest police station. Yet these very authorities seemed never to suspect that perhaps better street illumination could abate the problem.

A police car behind her flashed its red lights. The young woman panicked momentarily then cursed again softly because she had rather recently discovered that cursing was a balm. A little frightened, she thought of Al as she pulled to the side. "Oh, damn it!" she blinked nervously. What would she tell her husband Al?

The policeman stood a few feet from her window and aimed his flashlight beam on her face. She blinked again, turned away, and felt that she'd cry if he hassled her the slightest bit. What a night! Her research paper had received an unsatisfactory grade from her department head. The professor had looked terribly disappointed in her as he'd returned it tonight. He'd kept her after class and had calmly, systematically denigrated her senior thesis, and, thus, her ability, her promise. Then—rushing home late, with a broken fingernail, now bleeding. Now this. What would Al think?

"What's wrong with your lights, miss?" The police-man's voice was deep, all-business, but it wasn't harsh. She'd never been stopped by a cop before, primarily be-cause she hadn't been driving for very long.

She looked up at his wide, solemn face, the flashlight providing mere background lighting now that they'd each seen the other wasn't dangerous. "I don't understand," she muttered.

"Your headlights. They're off. Not working?"

"No, no...I..." She reached over, flipped the knob, and the black street winked into golden paleness. Her thoughts catapulted. "I—I just—"

The policeman leaned closer to the window. "What's wrong, miss?" He sensed her fear. "You've been crying. What's wrong?"

Her eyes overflowed. She felt so stupid. Stupid, stupid! She wouldn't have had to fumble for her keys if she'd taken them out before she left the professor's office. She wouldn't have forgotten her headlights if she hadn't been rushing so. Stupid! The tears flowed quite easily, as she knew what Al would say.

"I—it's just that I didn't have time to turn my lights on," she said softly. Her voice trembled a bit near the end of the sentence.

The policeman still sensed fear. There was something

wrong here. And she was crying.

"You see," she continued, unthinkingly wiping her cheek with the broken-nail hand, "it was so dark in the parking lot." Her mind groped: failed paper, broken nail, waiting husband…and traffic ticket? She trembled. She had never been stopped by a cop, and she felt so stupid. "And a man…I could've been…it was so dark!"

In her helplessness, she leaned her face on the steering wheel and allowed the tears to come.

The policeman's bulk stiffened, concern evident in his posture. He flashed the light in her face again, stepped closer to her window, and ran the light up and down her blouse, onto her lap, lines of care creasing his forehead.

"What's your name, miss? Let me see your license."

She reached toward her purse. In the policeman's light, she saw clearly that her fingernail had broken off at the skin, and a thin line of blood had formed, tiny, shiny droplets that stained the white canvas of her purse as she touched it. It hadn't hurt as much at first, but now her nail throbbed. Her fingers trembled as she pulled the license from her wallet, trembled visibly as she handed it to the officer.

There was blood on the license. The officer's eyes widened, and he shone the light on her face again.

"Turn this way, miss," he said. "Let me see your face better."

The Heavens Weep for Us

There was blood on her cheek.

He stiffened, looked at her license again.

"Maria Gaytan," he said, looking conscientiously from the photo to the woman, then back again. A conscientious policeman didn't let any suspicious incidents off lightly.

"Miss Gaytan, something happened to you out there." He motioned his head toward the darkened parking areas of the campus. Maria sobbed softly. "I have to know what happened." His voice was authoritative, leaving no room for disagreement in any form. "You said there was a man."

Maria's eyes were wide as she and the officer looked intently at one another. He rested one hand on her door and put his other hand on her shoulder. "I have to know." The blood on her cheek was drying.

Maria closed her eyes and said it quickly, hoping that her statement's half-truth would ameliorate her situation. Was she getting cited for a misdemeanor?

"A man in the lot—he could have assaulted me..."

"And you wouldn't be the first!" the officer said. "It's been happening, you know."

"Yes, I know," she said. She remembered her thoughts as she'd driven down the dark street. She would laugh at the irony of it all if she weren't so frightened: the professor, the cop, the fine, her husband. She was more than an hour late already, and Al would be fuming, of course. She wanted so much to please him. She had to hurry home.

"Officer, I didn't turn my lights on because I was trying to get away—," she swallowed, "—from a man. I didn't want to be assaulted. That's all." She paused. "I don't get a ticket, do I?" Her husband had made out their monthly budget a few nights ago. This month was tight.

"I'll let you go as soon as I get details." He pulled out a small spiral pad. Maria stared at the pad in confusion.

"But what do you need to know?"

"We're getting all the information we can on these campus assaults." He looked hard at her and aimed the flashlight beam at the pad.

Maria panicked. "But—but what can I tell you?"

"Miss Gaytan, you were driving down a street with your headlights off. You could've caused an accident. You say you didn't turn on your lights because you were in a hurry to get away. You thought a man was going to assault you. You wouldn't be the first victim."

Maria looked at him in horror. What had she gotten herself into?

"Nine. Nine young women like yourself..." He ran the beam up and down her blouse. "—have been assaulted in the past two-and-a-half months. Nine!"

Maria began to sob again. What had she gotten herself into? She covered her face with both hands and tried to calm herself. The tears flowed unchecked. What could she do? Surely she couldn't tell the policeman she'd lied to him. Her mind raced, but all she could acknowledge clearly was her confusion.

"What did he look like?"

"It was dark," she said.

"He must've been close enough for you to think he was going to assault you." *And for me to jump into my car and drive off without lights,* she thought.

"He was of a medium build, a little on the short side," she said slowly, "with dark, wavy hair." She was startled to hear an almost exact description of Al.

The officer was writing pensively. "Did he say anything to you?"

Maria tried to be credible. Perhaps if her story didn't sound phony, she'd get off without a fine. "Yes, he said he was going to—get me." She felt embarrassed at the triteness of it.

"Get you?"

"Yes, that he—liked college girls."

"Umm." The policeman seemed convinced. He nodded. "Then did he do anything?"

"Why, no," Maria stammered.

"Then why did you think he was going to assault you?"

"Because of what he said to me!" she shot back. Her tears came again. Her story was falling apart. What if he caught her in her lie? What did cops do to liars? "And...and..."

"Yes?" His pen stood poised. Maria stared at the spirals on the notepad. "What did he do?"

"He ran toward me," she blurted. She almost sobbed as she said, "Why else would I have hurried away? What else could have frightened me?"

She broke down completely. Her shoulders shook, and the steering wheel was quite damp from her tears. The cop opened her car door, gently helped her out, and reached in to get her purse. He held her by the arm, pushed down the lock button on the door.

"You're coming with me, Miss Gaytan."

She wailed. "No, no, I can't! My husband…."

The cop understood perfectly. How many of the other victims hadn't wanted to report the crimes at first because of shame, because women somehow had this terribly-misguided notion that they would thereafter be deemed un-chaste by the men, husbands or lovers, in their lives? Women could be so irrational sometimes. Maria didn't want her husband to find out. It was S.O.P. for female assault victims to want to shield their men from this degrada-tion. This girl was holding back, he knew, but the more they could get on these campus assailants, the better. These women needed time, that's all: time to build up the courage to tell all. Maybe at the station, Maria would spill all the beans.

Throughout the three-mile ride, Maria sat scrunched in

her corner and wept. She'd left her cell phone at home, so she couldn't call Al even if she'd wanted to. She clutched her handbag, not noticing that the tighter she clutched, the larger the droplets of blood that oozed from her fingertip. The blood soaked into the fabric, as ink would on a blotter, and spread slowly.

She'd been married to her medium-build-slightly-on-the short-side-wavy-haired husband for less than two years. She didn't quite know, as he didn't know now, why they'd married, really. They were both young, barely eighteen, when they'd wed in an unassuming home ceremony. They'd just completed high school and had been obsessed with their amazing sexual forays long into the night whenever her parents went out, as they frequently liked to do. But her puritan streak had demanded marriage; his apathetic/brusque character had been caught in an apathetic moment, and he'd acquiesced. So now she went to the local university, he worked as common laborer for a local construction firm, and they just scraped along.

After almost nineteen months of marriage, youthful sexuality waned, financial worries waxed. Al—no one ever called him Albert—resented her for her naiveté, her helplessness, her lack of financial independence. He drank regularly, criticized her endlessly. Thus, his sanity maintained by these dual safety-release valves, he went to work each morning, and she headed for school. In the evenings she had one class, tonight's class; and Al stayed home, drinking but not drunk, hungry, waiting for Maria to come home and feed him.

Maria thought of how Al had allowed her to remain in school because her parents had agreed to pay most of the tuition but primarily because she was an industrious student: not bright, but industrious. She was his "potential ticket to a rosy future," he'd often told her. If he saw tonight's red-marked senior thesis, thought Maria, and knew about her professor's disappointment....She wept harder.

And the louder she sobbed, the more concerned the policeman became. This girl wasn't telling everything!

The four men on duty at the police station hardly looked up when Maria and the cop walked in. A secretary glanced briefly at the pair as they walked up to her desk, then looked intently at Maria's handbag, still clutched tightly to her heaving bosom.

"Oh, my God!" the secretary said as she rose slowly. "You're hurt!"

Maria continued weeping, and the cop noticed her canvas purse for the first time. The blood stain was larger than a silver dollar. He looked at Maria's face more closely. Streaked blood covered both sides of her face now.

"Jesus!" he gasped. He held her hand, looked with grave concern at her now-swollen, still-bleeding finger. *Stupid!* Maria thought as she looked at her hand. *I'm so stupid. How many ways can I hurt myself?*

"Did he do that to you?" asked the officer in a low, husky voice. "Did he do that to you, Maria?" Fatherly concern obliterated objective formality.

The secretary dabbed at the girl's finger with a Kleenex, all the while murmuring soothing inanities, and two cops in an adjacent cubicle came toward Maria.

"What is it, Briskin?" one asked.

"She was assaulted on the university campus," answered the officer. They nodded sympathetically, looked at the sobbing coed. "You need to tell us more, Maria," said Briskin as he bent closer to her face.

"How did it happen?" asked the other officer.

"What else did the bastard do?" said the third cop.

"Did he do this?" Briskin asked Maria again.

She could barely speak. Her entire body shook, and the secretary tenderly hugged Maria.

"You must give us more details," said Briskin gently. She looked at him with wide eyes brimming, lips wet and quivering, face an irrefutable mask of fear. "How many other innocent women like yourself will end up victims?" Briskin emphasized each word, his face inching closer to Maria's with each word. "How did he hurt you?"

She sobbed, almost inaudibly. Her narrow shoulders moved up and down.

"He hurt you a lot, didn't he?" asked Briskin, his hand

on her left shoulder now.

"Yes!" she said clearly. "Yes, yes, I'm hurt! I'm so hurt! My husband...."

Briskin understood, and, thank God, the wall was slowly crumbling. This poor woman just needed a little tender, loving care, that's all. He placed his huge warm arm around her shoulders, and she turned toward him like a magnet meets a steel door. She clung to him, her chest pressing against his uniform, her arms entwined about his neck. Briskin was much concerned. The girl was falling apart. She needed protection, strong, male protection. Maybe the reassuring sight of her husband would encourage her to tell more, to see that her man's love would remain unchanged despite her trauma.

"I'm calling your husband," he announced to her reassuringly.

"My God! My God!" she screamed. He held her gingerly, soothed her, understood her turmoil.

"Yes, I think he should know everything that's happened tonight." He turned to the secretary. "And, Gertrude, call the hospital and tell them we're bringing in an assault victim for examination."

Maria forced herself away from Briskin. She was wild-eyed, totally uncontrollable. She lunged for the phone, tried to pull out the cord, cut her arm against an open metal desk drawer. It took three cops to restrain her. Her arm began bleeding. In her struggle, blood was smeared on her clothes and face.

Maria thought of her husband, of the story in the papers, of her professor, of the small, hot needles stabbing her fingertip, of the slow trickle of blood on her arm near the elbow. She thought all this, but only vaguely, for fear and confusion constricted her brain, made it feel as if a tight metal band were clamped around her skull.

I'm hurt. I'm stupid. I'm so hurt.

When Al walked into the police station twenty-five minutes later, his face was a chalky embodiment of concern and bewilderment. He spotted Maria cowering in a corner by the water fountain. Briskin hovered near her. Maria was disheveled, blood-stained, wild-eyed, and was biting her knuckles in panic.

"Maria!" her husband cried and stretched out his arms toward her like he hadn't done in months. "Oh, Maria!"

She tremulously got to her feet and stared helplessly at him as he approached her. Her eyes were round, terrible.

"Al!" she blurted as he came and touched her face. "Oh, Al! I've been raped!"

Juana Macho

They say that in a crisis, the body goes into overdrive, adrenaline flowing so hard, body and mind tear away from one another and maybe never reconnect.

Juana Macho

1

"Juana! Juana Macho!"

The husky man in the green plaid shirt, sleeves rolled up above his elbows, held four opened beer bottles in his large hands. He meandered his way between and around the throng at the bar and the stompers dancing on the small wood stage directly in front of the bar. He was glad to see Juana in the jukebox corner of the cantina and wasn't surprised she didn't respond. The noise level could split eardrums in a matter of minutes.

"Hey, *muchacha*!" he tried again as he got closer to his old friend. She looked up when he plunked the bottles firmly on the small table, their clinking inaudible. He slapped her on the back and she reached out a calloused hand to shake his. She half-rose from the table, a man's gesture in the presence of a woman, but the friend was seated in a second.

Juana's face was pitted with scars, most noticeably shiny, pink patches and crinkled brown swaths across her nose, forehead, and the tops of her cheeks. Her jaw was square, firm, yet somehow feminine. Some of the scars were faint, raised welts, particularly one that ran from below her left eye to the edge of her mouth. This gave her a crooked smile, one of her well-known physical characteristics in the small, dusty Texas town she'd recently moved into and adopted as her own.

"*Cabrón!*" she cursed playfully at him as she slapped him on the chest and gave him a small push. "Well, there goes the neighborhood now that you're here!" Her voice was a scratchy tenor, her laugh a deep snort. She lifted one of her friend's beer bottles, without invitation, and took a long swig. Her fingers around the neck of the bottle were brown, thick, wrinkled beneath the crisp sleeves of her black shirt.

"*Cabrona!*" he responded with a smile. He tipped his NY Yankees cap back on his head and leaned strong elbows on the table. He noticed for the first time that Juana wasn't wearing her cowboy hat. He narrowed his eyes, studied her face and head carefully, all the while drinking slowly from one of the fresh beers. He didn't remember the last time he'd seen her bare-headed. Her salty-peppered hair was cropped close, sideburns buzz-cut, gel making the tops and sides of her hair resemble small porcupine quills. This was a new look, to be sure. A new look for Juana. He tried to think of how many years ago he'd last seen her.

"New town, new hair, huh?" he yelled into her ear. The noise was still incredible. She hadn't changed colognes, he noticed. Still the strong musky scent she'd worn for years. He wore it, too. In fact, she'd bought a bottle for him a long time ago, then had started using the cologne herself. The thumping music from the jukebox near them reverberated in his chest as he drank slowly. Juana moved her head up and down with the music's beat, her eyes scanning the dance floor, the bar, constantly shifting and alert.

"Hey, Macho!" he said to her, hoping that this would swing her attention back to him. "Don't you want to know why I'm here? How I ran across you?"

She squinted at him, shook her head. He repeated his question in her ear, and she straightened up, squinted at him again, and shook her head. She didn't want to know.

"Well, I'll tell you anyway," he shouted. He was practically in her lap now. "I heard you were here. It's not hard to track you down." He wasn't a stalker, she knew. She wasn't concerned that her old friend had tracked her down. He kept his arm around the back of her chair, his mouth close to her ear. "I wanted to see you again."

She pulled back and stared into his face. She finished

her bottle of beer and took a deep, long draught of a second one. Then she rose, swaggered to a table of women nearby, spoke briefly to one of them. Juana took the giggling woman's hand and walked her to the dance platform. She brought the woman in close to her body, placed her head against the woman's hair, and began swaying sensually to the rhythm of the music, eyes closed.

2

It was almost three in the morning when Juana pulled into her driveway. She was alone, having completed her carousing at the old honky-tonk after midnight and continuing at that woman's house in a nearby town. Juana stumbled a bit on the gravel in her driveway. It was especially dark tonight, and, without any lighting in her yard, it was always difficult to navigate the narrow, bumpy driveway, by car or by foot. The beers she'd had weren't helping either. She fumbled with the keys and let herself into her house.

Juana had moved into this wooden shack almost two years ago. It was remote, surrounded by mesquite trees, cacti, and scrub brush. There was nothing attractive about the property, but it was ample enough for her, and it was cheap enough and isolated enough that it met her needs. It was a remnant of an old ranch that had flourished decades prior. Now the acre or so, with the wooden-post-and-

barbed-wire fence marking its boundaries jaggedly, sat
desolately at the outskirts of a god-forsaken piddle of a
town called Dominguez. But living here met Juana's needs,
so who could ask for more?

Her needs had dictated that she leave Laredo, a mish-
mash city that cared and didn't care. Like a gypsy with too
many secrets to hide, Juana had moved from her hometown, her birthplace, to three different cities, including
Laredo, then eventually to smaller and smaller towns when
her secrets weren't so important to hide anymore. Now, at
the age of forty, she found herself in this dusty, dessicated
corner of Texas: without family, without friends, without
any connections from her past, which was how she liked it.

Until tonight.

Damn Manuel!

Oh yeah, she'd noticed him when he first walked in.
She'd seen him despite the throng of sweating, laughing
bodies massed near the doorway and throughout the cantina. She saw him as he scanned the crowds and had half-
hoped he was seeking her. Her heart had slid into her stomach when he started wending his way toward her dusky
corner. He'd not spoken to anyone along the way, had not
looked at any woman. He was a man on a mission, and her
heart remained pitted in her stomach as she realized that
she—Juana Macho—was his mission.

"Damn you, Manuel!" she said aloud now as she undressed in the dark. She'd been cool, convincingly detached...or so she hoped now as she wondered whether or not she'd been convincing enough. After she danced with that woman, she'd lingered in another dark corner with her, standing close to her body, her calloused hands on the woman's waist. She had the routine down pat. She knew how to deal with these women after all these years.

Manuel had waited for her at the small table for about ten minutes. He'd drunk his beer then finished off the remaining bottle. He'd glanced several times in Juana's direction but never rose from his chair until he rose to leave. He exited the back way, not looking at any woman along the way. As she saw him leaving, Juana's heart remained in her stomach. To her chagrin, it remained trapped and smothered there for the rest of the night.

In her cotton nightgown now, Juana slid into her dark bed and pulled the covers around her neck though the night was warm outside. Juana wept herself to sleep.

3

The dream was brief. Her dreams were that way now.

When Juana Macho was a teenager, the dreams tormented her for years. Recurring dreams, scenes that shook her awake in the middle of the night, or bathed her in a dampness that shivered her awake too early in the morning.

The Heavens Weep for Us

The house that she never recognized, with unpainted, splintered boards bare inside and out. The emptiness that clothed the house as she floated room through interminable vacant room. The kitchen, rocking violently back and forth as on a ship, walls colored deep red, feeling slippery and cold. Then explosions, always two explosions, and her body lifted to the ceiling of the wretched house, glowing, glowing, sputtering and spitting, spinning in a black cloud that never settled, never opened, never cleared.

But those dreams had worn themselves away years ago, worn themselves into snapshots of those terrors. Little scenes, little horrors, explosions muffled, then poofed away, the dream ending abruptly. This was how a grown woman dreamt, a grown woman who'd used up her stock of fear, a grown woman who'd dried her eyes out pretty well in hundreds of nights. Juana Macho was grateful for the passage of years.

Yet she remembered. Of course she remembered what happened. They say that in a crisis, the body goes into overdrive, adrenaline flowing so hard, body and mind tear away from one another and maybe never reconnect. They call it shock. They call it God-given amnesia. They call it a blessing from up high that allows folks to outlive their horror. But it didn't happen that way for Juana Macho. She was eleven and shouldn't have been alone at home. But school was out, and her mother had just taken a quick run to the store, just a quick run. Juanita Maria was alone at home and hungry, and it had not been the first time. She lived in the sticks, in a place that should've been torn down years ago. When the little girl named Juanita Maria Camacho put the match to that stove, neighbors in the next block heard the explosion.

4

As Manuel left the cantina that night, he'd been angry, but not too angry. He'd grown accustomed to her doing that to him. Dominguez, Laredo, San Antonio, and who knows where else. Texas was a wide-open hiding place for her, had been a hide-and-seek quandary for him for years now. He'd grown accustomed to her flee-and-fetch.

Except that she didn't want to be fetched. Didn't want to be found, to be caught. As a man, he had grown to understand this.

He was just a kid when the explosion happened. Her classmate, her best friend, the little boy who sat behind Juanita Maria Camacho and twirled her long, glossy curls in his fingers while she tried to smother her giggles. The little boy who drew airplanes, boats, trains for her. The little boy who fantasized with her about how these planes and ships could take them to the land of the sphinx and to the place in Italy where houses stood on water. The little boy who also had no brothers or sisters, the little boy who also didn't live in the northeast part of town and who also didn't have nice clothes. The little boy who lived across the street from her, so near and so far. They were the proverbial peas in a pod.

Manuel knew he couldn't go to Juanita Maria's house to play. Parents didn't let anyone in, and they didn't let her out. He knew his best friend was alone at home a lot. Knew she cleaned house, nursed her alcoholic father, hid secrets for her mother. When he allowed Juanita Maria into his heart, Manuel knew the depth of the aloneness the little girl carried in hers. He accepted her isolation and tried to mesh his isolation with hers, so that two broken child-hearts could possibly become one whole one.

And for the five years he sat in classrooms with her, Manuel and Maria Juanita slowly wove their friendship into something that could withstand the emptiness of home. Quiet, pensive: there was something spiritual about Juanita Maria that even a little boy could understand. The day the two eleven-year-olds sat underneath the giant oak tree at school, eating sandwiches from reused brown bags, reciting the ancient wonders of the world they'd see together when they grew up... the day of the explosion....Well, this was a day Manuel would never forget.

He pulled his navy blue Jeep into his apartment complex. Kingsville, his hometown now, was forty miles away from Dominguez. When he left the cantina tonight without saying goodbye to Juana, he felt abandoned, demeaned. How could she do that to him? No. How, after all these years of his protestations to her, could she *still* do that to him?

He entered his small but well-appointed home long before midnight, which meant he had a few hours still left for dwelling on Juana, on the tremulous joy he had felt in finding her. Dwelling on the fear in his legs and arms, in his pulsing forehead, as he'd walked to her corner in the cantina tonight. Recalling his pleasure as he placed his mouth close to her face and wrapped his arm around her back along the edge of the chair.

He took a Pepsi from his fridge and slumped into an overstuffed chair. He drank slowly, remembering a few other things from tonight, a few more items to dwell on: the gray in her hair, the way her eyes avoided his for most of their brief encounter, the thickness in her wrinkled fingers, and especially....He shifted uneasily, flicked on the TV to calm his thoughts.

The way she rubbed against that woman, how Juana held her close, her face almost lost in the woman's long brown hair. Manuel rubbed his temples in big, slow circles, his eyes closed, as he tried to erase the image from his mind. But then a bigger pain grabbed him, and the recollection of his own actions many years ago reached even more deeply, stabbed more cruelly, and he sank more heavily into his chair at the thought of it.

As a teenager, Manuel had run across Juana while visiting relatives in San Antonio, more than one hundred miles away. It was fate, he thought then. "It was fate," he said aloud now, still convinced that the gods had always meant for them to remain bonded to one another, though that first encounter after her departure was pained and horrid. Who would have guessed that two people who'd been apart, totally without communication for three years, would literally trip into one another in a place neither had visited before?

Manuel rubbed his face absent-mindedly as he recalled the faraway scene. He had not seen the effects of the fire on his beloved classmate. In truth, her parents allowed nobody but Juanita Maria's doctors near her when she returned home. The girl had been taken to a hospital in another town, far away from visitors of any sort. Her parents cloistered her more excessively than ever, and Juanita Maria became more invisible as the months wore on. The last time he glimpsed his friend was the day a brown hauling truck pulled in front of her house, and her parents piled their shabby belongings into it. Unceremoniously, they left town, Juanita Maria shrouded in a long, gray coat and floppy hat, just as she'd been when she had returned home from the hospital.

So when Manuel bounded down the grassy hill in that

faraway park in San Antonio years later, he tripped on someone unknown: a boy? a girl? He couldn't tell. They tangled on the slope of the lawn momentarily, then the trampled youth stood up: baggy khakis, baggy flannel shirt, long-sleeved though it was summertime, men's shoes, baseball cap pulled low, wisps of black hair peeking timidly from underneath the canvas cap. When the youth looked up at Manuel, Manuel was stunned:

Juanita Maria Camacho. Beautiful Juanita Maria.

Scarred. Disfigured. Solemn.

Manuel's silence was heart-rending to the girl. She had recognized him immediately and gazed at his face with clear recollections of what he had meant to her, clear remembrances of wondrous trips they had vowed to take together, lunches eaten in solidarity against the cruelties of childhood. She smiled at him with sheer joy in being with her friend again. She took a step toward him, hands outstretched. Pink, rubbery, scarred hands.

Manuel backed away stiffly, eyes glued to the girl's face, her hands. He said nothing to her. When she said his name, he remained silent, then turned quickly and ran toward the exit of the park.

In a Kingsville apartment, the forty-year-old Manuel, slouched in an easy chair by a flickering TV screen near midnight, remembered these things. He recalled all this with horror and shame, mostly shame at his horror.

5

Women are my solace. My only solace. When I lost my womanhood, I knew I had to grasp for it however I could. Can you imagine what it's like to not have breasts? To have hair that stops just there, no more? Patches of skin on my head where only stubble grows? Skin no man wants to kiss?

Juana Macho read aloud from her journal. She'd given up trying to sleep. She sat at her kitchen table, the bedcoverings wrapped around her shoulders, white nightgown scraping the floor beneath her shoeless feet. Though the bare bulb in the kitchen was too dim for proper reading, Juana had no trouble making out her words in her worn leatherette book. She had read them enough times, for many years now, these words from an alien being, from a familiar being, from someone she hated, from someone she sometimes loved.

Can you imagine a woman without softness? So the softness has to be found outside of me, beyond me, around me. I reach for it when I find it: a woman's softness, a woman's breasts, supple skin, gentle curves I've never had, pleasure denied me by flames and fury long, long ago. I reach for what I'm not. I behold and hold what I cannot find in myself.

Juana imagined herself explaining these things to

Manuel. She read the words aloud, haltingly but with sincerity.

Men seek this softness as well. They won't find it in me. You won't find it in me, Manuel. Men seek beauty. You'll see none in me, Manuel.

She gazed from the book in her hand to the empty chair beside her, imagining her old friend at the table. Juana rose and set her book down hesitantly. She walked to her bedroom, let the heavy bedcoverings drop away from her shoulders, removed the nightgown slowly, letting it, too, fall to her feet. She stepped to the skinny mirror behind the bathroom door and pulled aside the curtain she had tacked over the glass. She positioned the glass so she could see all of her, head to toe, despite the fact that she had kept only the nightlight on in the cramped room. Courage only stretched so far.

The flames had been merciless. How she survived was a story her parents never cared to unearth. Juana recalled the excruciating pain, the chalk-faces of the men who ran to slap their jackets on her burning body, and their red, yelling mouths. As she rolled on the dirt amidst the chaos, she'd been amazed at the blueness of the sky, the brilliance of the sun, and had marveled momentarily at how the black plumes rising from her house had split the sky so neatly.

Now look at what the flames did to that little girl: her skin from forehead to toes was puckered and welted. The different colors pocked throughout her body spoke to the varying degrees of damage: deep brown across her chest, resembling a tight elastic band that obliterated any semblance of womanhood, pink across the inner thighs, coarse brown across the front and back of her legs. Her hands: permanently discolored, fingernails blunted. Her feet:...

Juana sank to the linoleum floor and sobbed. She shouldn't have done this, shouldn't have looked. She rarely saw herself. She made a point of this. She had no other mirrors in the house and avoided all mirrors in public places. This mirror was in her home only because she had been unable to disattach it from the door, and her superstitious nature wouldn't allow her to break it. So she had covered it and only now foolishly uncovered it. For what purpose?

Her head was on the bare floor now. She sobbed as she made her explanation aloud to Manuel, to her fantasy friend who had recoiled in horror many years ago and who had, from guilt no doubt, only from guilt, made feeble attempts to see her in the decades hence.

So you see now? You see why I can't have you?

She hugged herself on the floor, folded her legs as best as she could to her chest.

Do you understand now why I seek solace as I do?

She doubted that Manuel would ever come back. He had surely seen at the cantina last night that Juana was still a freak. A woman who dressed like a man, moved and spoke like a man, drank like a man, seduced like a man. A woman with a man's life but a woman's memory. How could she ever go back? How could she be what she was not for Manuel, yet continue to be what she was not for Juana?

Her keening could have awakened the dead. Only her wails the day of the fire surpassed the pain pouring forth now.

And Manuel heard it all.

Saw it all.

He couldn't sleep, so he had driven the forty miles back to Dominguez, had learned from the weary bartender where Juana Macho lived. If she wouldn't have him, at least he couldn't let the evening end without farewells.

He saw her with the book, saw from the darkness outside her window the desecrated body of his beloved friend. Saw her sink to the floor and weep. When he couldn't endure any more, he pushed the old front door open and went to retrieve her from her sorrow, as he should have done so very long ago. He picked her up and gently wrapped her in her bedcoverings. He soothed her spiky hair.

He had heard her words.

Sobbing into her neck, he could only say, over and over: "Juanita Maria, Juanita Maria."

Illusions

Millie plopped into the fat vinyl chair and swiveled it to face Beth. Millie beamed. Nobody got ten-dollar tips at this salon. Nobody!

Illusions

J ohnetta Lavenicia Tatu—Jonnie to most—walked into the beauty school salon for only the second time in her life. Her flowered dress hung loosely about her tall frame, and she held herself erect at the counter. Her chocolate face was smooth, plain, serene despite the burning sore at the nape of her neck that had brought her back into the shop. Her hand touched the area around the sore gingerly as she waited for the clerk at the counter to finish with the client ahead of Jonnie.

"Yeah," said the clerk finally, after looking up at Jonnie and determining that this customer was not anybody she needed to impress.

"I need to see someone about my neck," said Jonnie, her accent immediately announcing her newness in the country. She held her hand just under her scruff, her voice as calm as if she had just asked the clerk the time of day.

"Mr. John!" called out the clerk and waited for the salon manager to come forward. After a few minutes of staring past Jonnie, the clerk leaned toward the ruddy, curly-headed man who approached the desk briskly. The clerk pointed to the tall woman.

"My, my, my!" clucked Mr. John as he inspected Jonnie's neck. Jonnie had obviously had to cut away a two-inch swatch of hair at her nape to allow the sore to ventilate. It was at least two inches across, very red around the uneven edges, and still seeping fluid despite a dark scab that had formed over its center. Jonnie's face did not change expression as Mr. John lifted her hair gingerly and prodded around the edges of the wound.

"Who worked on you?" he asked her.

"It was Tina, I believe," the woman replied hesitantly. She seemed to be choosing her words carefully, gazing steadily at Mr. John. "She did a nice job, really, sir, a real nice job, and I liked my hair. Yes, sir, I did, but then this happened, and...."

Mr. John pursed his lips and continued examining the sore, shaking his head. "Hmm. Hair relaxer?"

"Yes," Jonnie said, looking straight ahead as the man, shorter than Jonnie, squinted ever more closely at her neck. Jonnie smiled faintly, scanning the salon and wondering if Tina would be in trouble over this. This possibility made Jonnie uncomfortable.

The Heavens Weep for Us

"Well, we're gonna take care of this and not even charge you," said Mr. John. He took Jonnie's arm and led her toward one of the fifteen lavender-and-pink work stations. By this time, several of the hairdressers had ceased their work and were staring at Jonnie as she followed the pudgy manager past the stations.

"Poor Tina," muttered one of the employees. She stared momentarily at Jonnie's retreating figure, remembered her client, then continued snipping away at the woman's newly-bleached hair.

The new blonde had hardly noticed her hairdresser's lapse. She leaned back in the vinyl chair, her eyes closed as if in sleep, her body totally relaxed, hands hanging loosely over the sides of the chair arms, legs thrown open in such a way that only the long drape that protected her clothes held them somewhat together at the knees. As the hairdresser snipped ever more precariously toward the woman's ears, the blonde's legs almost imperceptibly inched farther apart, their owner immersed in reverie.

Her crotch twitched. Todd's hand was sliding up her leather skirt just as smoothly as she knew it would be when he got around to it. Lord only knew why it had taken him so long to seduce her. She'd been wanting him since he'd begun picking up his mail at her UPS store a few months prior. Tonight, after the requisite wine and progressively-intimate dinner conversation, he'd finally gotten around to it—to *it,* twitching madly now, more than ever since Ray, twitching and heating up in pace with Todd's breathing. *You're so damn beautiful!* he was saying. *You have no idea how long I've been wanting to do this to you.* She damn well *did* have an idea, and she wanted him to hurry and get to *it.* Her legs slowly spread apart.

"Ouch!" As the blood trickled down her earlobe, the blonde's legs snapped together, and she jerked upright. A few drops landed on the drape. The hairdresser stared open-mouthed at the red tips of her scissors and flushed deeply. Was anyone watching? She grabbed a gob of cotton and dabbed at the woman's ear as the latter blinked rapidly to keep the tears in.

"I'm so sorry, so very, very sorry," whispered Millie, the hairdresser, over and over. In her distress, she'd dropped the scissors on the tiled checkerboard floor, and it was this *clunk!* that caught the attention of the adjacent hairdressers. She was horrified. What would Mr. John say?

She and the blonde eventually stanched the flow of blood sufficiently enough to begin treating the nicked ear-lobe. First, the alcohol with its attendant elicitations of sucked breath and clenched eyes. Then, the bandage, fished from the bottom drawer, where Mr. John had admonished them all to keep the bandages. ("You never know when you'll need these, but let's keep them out of sight so you'll be reminded that we don't *want* to need them," he'd told them during their training.) Finally, the bedside manner—also part of their beauty college training—the soothing murmurs and sustained apologies that eventually got the blonde to unclench her eyes.

Ray. The blonde gazed at her reflection in the rococo mirror, the present crisis having unrelaxed her, her usual stuffiness returning to her demeanor. Wounded ear aside, Todd would never see her sexiness. She was, after all, probably twelve years older than he. She hated the fluorescent lights over the tall, fake-gild mirrors. She hated the blotches on her skin, remnants of a few dermabrasion treatments gone awry. Her crow's feet were not all that noticeable, thanks to botox, but she knew Todd would never tell her she was beautiful, never take her to dinner, and that she'd never have to spread her legs in his presence. If only he could *see* her sensuality, if he could *sense* it, like Ray had.

Ray. The blonde sighed, slumped slowly into the vinyl, shut her eyes once more, and slowly began to spread her legs apart as the hairdresser, heaving a sigh, tried to even out the hair on the other side.

"You okay there, Millie?" The beautician to the left of the haircutter's station had silently watched the proceedings with the blonde. She ate lunch daily with Millie, just the two of them sitting on the farthest bench out on the back patio of the salon, away from the guffaws of the other employees. Millie liked Beth and glanced over at her now with a tired smile.

"Yeah, thanks."

Beth returned the smile with an almost identical one and didn't look at Millie again for the next half-hour. Millie churned. It took an immense effort for her to keep her hands steady. She was grateful that the blonde had gone back to sleep, or, at least, she seemed to be asleep. She must be sure not to stir her again until she'd done the job and done it well.

You won't make it, Milo, her mother had told Millie upon hearing the news that her only daughter was leaving for California. *You ain't cut out to be no beautician! Who on earth fooled you that you was? What's getting into you?* Her mother had stirred the potatoes on the stove energetically, frowning all the while, wiping her sweaty brow and glancing with tight lips at her twenty-five-year-old daughter. Millie had held menial jobs after struggling through high school, had never married nor been engaged, had hardly dated, had lived with her widowed mother, alone, since grade school, and had hardly ventured out of Kansas. On the day of her announcement to her mother, her day of freedom, this was how her mother had greeted what Millie had thought would be welcome news. *You won't make it.*

Still, Millie had packed. She'd reluctantly pulled the posters of her favorite movie stars off the striped walls of her bedroom, had slowly rolled them up, each one lovingly, and had not had the heart to dump them in the bin behind their porch, leaving them instead at her teenage neighbor's door on her way out of town. On the bus ride to the coast, Millie had read glamour magazines, three or four gossip tabloids, a copy of the *Los Angeles Times* that she'd picked up in Las Vegas, the thrilling highlight of her trek, and had mailed a postcard to her mother from Bakersfield. It had taken Millie days to adjust to her freedom. For the first eleven nights away from home, she'd watched television in her motel room till sign-off, forcing her eyelids open, hoping that the dryness, the effort, would preclude tears. In the land of sunshine and forever-fame, Millie had not freed herself.

"Haven't you done enough now?"

"No," Millie replied absent-mindedly. She glanced quickly into the mirror and saw, in a flash of embarrassment, that her client had spoken to her.

"Well, I think you've done enough now," said the blonde, tugging at the wisps around her ears. Her eyes were slightly puffy from having been closed so long. She looked at Millie in the mirror and noticed that the girl had again turned deep red. "Is this your first haircut?"

"Oh, no," stammered Millie. "No, no, not at all. Haircuts are my specialty. I've put in over a hundred hours. It's my one...it's my main area of expertise." Her face was still flushed, but she felt proud of her response. She sounded professional.

"Well, you *have* done a nice job," said the blonde half-heartedly. She pursed her lips—Millie was reminded of her mother at the stove that day—as she fished in her handbag for the tip. She pulled out a crisp ten-dollar bill and handed it nonchalantly to Millie. The blonde remembered for an instant that this was the last of her lunch allowance for the week, but it was too late: the hairdresser had already taken it from her and put it into her smock. The blonde took a deep breath to compose herself, stood up, straightened the faux-suede skirt over her broad thighs, and walked as majestically as she could toward the front counter.

Millie plopped into the fat vinyl chair and swiveled it to face Beth. Millie beamed. Nobody got ten-dollar tips at this salon. Nobody! Beth dusted off her client and smiled briefly at Millie before sweeping the long red hairs of her previous patron into the plastic dustpan. Beth hated Millie. She hated the fact that she, Beth, was the newest kid on the block and had not yet been accepted into any of the salon cliques, that the only person willing to give her the time of day was Millie. So she ate lunch with her day after day, listening to endlessly-redundant tales of Kansas, droning descriptions of Millie's dead father, and pitiful recitations of Millie's dreams: empty, empty, empty. And now here was Millie with a crisp ten-dollar tip after having butchered that poor woman's hair, and she herself? Well, all she'd gotten from her red-haired mistress was two bucks. There was no justice in this world.

"Beth?"

Tina, in the station immediately behind Beth's, had leaned over in the space between the tall, standing mirrors attached to each separate adjacent table, or "station," as the salon jargon went. Beth straightened, surprised, as she saw Tina's polished face. Tina was the pariah of the day, this was true, because of the way she'd carelessly burned the Black woman's neck. But normally Tina was one of the most popular hairdressers in the salon. In the two months that Beth had worked here, Tina had never spoken to her by name. This was an interesting development indeed. Beth gave Tina her most ingratiating smile and looked at her expectantly.

"Beth, got any Vaseline?"

Beth did. She handed it delicately to her new friend and returned to her sweeping with a new energy.

Tina was disgusted. Jonnie had been her first Black customer ever, and even on that day, she'd not wanted to do her. Tina didn't understand Black people's hair, and Jonnie's hair had been particularly coarse, uncooperative. All the coaxing in the world had not gotten her hair to curl just so, or to lie flat in places it was meant to do so, and to fluff at just the right spots. Now, Tina had to deal with this ugly sore on this Black neck. It still had pus in it, for heaven's sake! She slipped on her latex glove—she *never* wore gloves except for chemical work!—so she could rub Vaseline on the woman's neck without puking. As she dipped her forefinger into Beth's jar, Tina looked into the mirror and smiled sweetly at Jonnie, who smiled back shyly.

"I'm so terribly sorry this happened," said Tina. "I promise you that it's the first time I've ever done this to any of my clients." Of course. She'd never done a Black client before.

Jonnie gazed at Tina. "Don't worry about it, miss," she said softly. "A little pain don't never killed nobody."

Tina inwardly winced. God, what a chore it was to put up with ignorant people! Yet there was something about this salon that attracted a goodly share of—how would Tina say it?—"under-sophisticated patrons." Without having to look around, Tina knew what it was: she'd always detested the wavy linoleum floor, the resin mirrors with their cobwebbed corners, the vinyl upholstery ("faux leather," as Mr. John called it), and faded drapes that had probably at one time been "over the top" fancy. Even Mr. John, that outdated peacock, belonged in the category of grotesqueness that so marked this salon. What airs he put on! He'd had his straight, thinning hair permed yesterday by that pet of his, Beth. Whom did he think he was deceiving anyway? Plumping up his hair with gobs of mousse, thinking that the curls and the mousse made his hair look thicker! He was beyond help. Everybody at this salon hated Mr. John, with his polyester pants and potbelly jiggling as he strutted from station to station, insisting on infallibility. Had he forgotten how he'd scorched a patron's ear last month when he was using a faulty curling iron? And how could he not tell—he, Mr. John!—that the damn curling iron was kaput?

And of course, everybody hated Beth because she obviously was Mr. John's pet.

Lost in thought, Tina completed her job on Jonnie with hardly any notice of having done so. She straightened out Jonnie's haircut at the scruff, made sure the sore was properly treated and protected, and generally made the woman feel like new again. When Jonnie rose from the chair, her smooth face was radiant.

"Let me take a final look," said Mr. John, as he walked crisply up to Jonnie before she finished dusting herself off. "Umm. Looks great. Just great." He turned to Tina and smiled generously at her. "You've redeemed yourself. Did a super mop-up job here." Turning to Jonnie: "Tell me, pretty lady. How do you feel now?"

"I feel no pain. My hair looks good. Believe me, sir, I'm very happy with you all's work today." Jonnie's grin was totally genuine.

Mr. John patted Tina on her shoulder, and Tina bent over lightly and pecked him on the cheek before he wheeled away. She turned to give Jonnie the full benefit of her smile.

Jonnie did not move for several seconds, recollecting something important. She did not have any money with her. Back in the old country, her mother had oftentimes told her: *Johnetta Lavenicia Tatu. You got a million-dollar name, honey, but don't never forget that life ain't easy. You may never have much else to your name but your name.* Today Jonnie didn't have money, so she couldn't give Tina a tip. Jonnie's face remained smooth, serene, so indubitably childlike, that only she knew the deep embarrassment she felt as she told Tina this.

"I thank you with my heart," she said simply to Tina, "because it's all I can do." She nodded her head politely to Tina, finished dusting herself off, and walked slowly, regally toward the front door. Tina immediately began sweeping the floor and straightening up her station to hide her disappointment and humiliation.

From across the salon, from the balcony on the mezzanine where Mr. John watched all his charges like the proverbial hawk, he watched Tina stooping, sweeping, dusting. It was too late. Burning people's necks was inexcusable.

He would fire Tina tomorrow.

Saving Up

Our memories crowd us sometimes. Too many memories sometimes. Too sharp, or too fuzzy sometimes. Unbalanced, sometimes.

Saving Up

You may not remember it the way I do, dearest Pablo, but when we danced naked in our bedroom to Gato Barbieri's *Europa* on the night of our fifth anniversary, I was weeping, hoping my hair all wild around my cheeks and shoulders would soak the tears and you wouldn't feel them on your neck. You hugged me so tightly, *mi amor*, and you hummed the tune—that haunting, soulful tune we loved so much—with your eyes seamed so securely, I think now that you probably wouldn't have noticed my tears anyway. The music wrapped us both, your thick thighs pushing between my legs, my damp breasts almost flat against your chest and arms. When the music stopped, you peeled yourself away from me just long enough to push the button on the stereo again, then folded me into your warmth once more, and we danced and danced on our old, beige rug ten, twelve, fourteen times before we fell, eyes closed fiercely but gently, onto the bed and lay there silently, hearts racing. When you put your lips on mine, our legs entwined, Gato's music still flowed, still wailed its sensous heartbreak into our limbs, weaving us together, and for hours we could not sleep.

Do you remember that, *mi corazón?*

Now I can tell you that I wept for the moment. I wept for eternity and for the fleetingness of things. Dear God, I prayed, let this night be carved into the tiniest corners of my brain. Let me not forget his smell, his muscles, his most private hairs, the spotlets of sweat on his mouth, how he's sewn his flesh to mine, how he's mine, mine, mine, for five years and for fifty more. My rapture that night, dear Pablo, was touched with sadness that our bodies someday would be putty, that this energy coursing in our veins would someday be stilled, and the memory of Gato and our anniversary would be all that we could hold.

And remember when our son was born? How could six pounds of downy flesh have caused such havoc? When we arrived at the ward, you settled into that old recliner in the corner of the hospital room, remote control in hand, and switched channels on the television set bolted high into the wall, glancing at me every now and then. When the contractions came, you bolted from the comfort of your corner to give me comfort of your own: clumsy, halting, anxious comfort, but you'll never know how the scratchy touch of your hands on my belly, the beads perched on your fore-head belying your façade of being unflustered, gave me calm. Your brow wrinkled, voice silky as you could mus-ter, and your moist eyes flashed what your heart really felt, the fear of first fatherhood palpable. And when our boy ar-rived, your joy could not be eclipsed. How I loved that day!

Saving up. I didn't know it then, but I'd started saving up.

Photos can be lost or burned or stolen or thrown away. They can be forgotten when one moves from home to home, in the bustle of gathering the trappings of our lives for transport to another context, where these trappings will be re-arranged to redefine who and what we are in a crazy quest to capture our lives. But memories...

Do you recall, Pablo *mi rey*, when you built our home, built it with your own hands, my love, your own hands long into the night when you'd come home from working at the station? No house was good enough for us, poor as we were, but you meant that no house was built to soothe our souls, to be the backdrop for what our lives would cre-ate. You wanted the windows to be where we wanted them to be, to choose the trees or streets, the exact corner of the sky and clouds that we wanted our eyes to fall on when we looked outside. You wanted a certain patch of ground (for me) beside the kitchen window, another special square of little earth for our boy's frolics, and you wanted to be master of our crafted world. You hewed those beams, pillars, windowsills, wooden floors, little porches to envelop our moments with security. The sight of you straddling the roof rafters, working alone, nails in your lips, pencil on your ear, hammer pounding the blue air in that special corner of the town you chose for us: all this is etched into my memory.

Saving up.

Remember, Pablo, when you first took our boy into a swimming pool? It was a windy, hot night and we had stopped at that Arizona motel on our road trip to Texas. It was late, almost midnight, but we were all so filled with excitement, and the aqua waters shimmying in the kidney pool beckoned us mercilessly. Our little boy stood as tall as he could in the shallow end, determined to make his four-year-old body appear courageous and ready for independence. His alabaster face was a lamp, a radiant lamp with his fear and anticipation and little gasps whenever his mouth touched the cold water. You lifted him, floated him on his back, carried him on your horsey-back, and convinced him that he could swim. And he did! As I watched from the lounge chair by the pool, my heart was too full to hold our joy, and—again—I wept.

I wept for the moment, *mi amor.*

The years are like tumbleweeds, aren't they? Tumbleweeds are rough, though, and thorny, ugly, and I don't mean to imply our lives have always been thus. But tumbleweeds gather so many little and big things, everything swirling together, blended into a ball of deceptive momentum that propels itself hither and yon, uncontrollably. In Arizona I was spellbound by the tumbleweeds. After we came in from the pool, I sat at the window and, while you both slept, I watched tumbleweeds crisscross that desert behind the motel until the first rays of day pushed me into bed for an hour or so until you awoke.

Our memories crowd us sometimes. Too many memories sometimes. Too sharp, or too fuzzy sometimes. Unbalanced, sometimes: painful, happy, then too many painful moments swarming in our heads. That's when I think of tumbleweeds and that Arizona night. The joy in the pool, the loneliness of the tumbleweeds. The uncertainty of our course. Those tumbleweeds tossing and turning in the hot wind.

I try not to remember the night you almost burned to death, and…. Even now—how many years later?—the tears spring. How could God have let us be blind for those few moments and not let us see the candle that fell from our bedroom windowsill? How could God have let us be wrapped in our joy, as we were till near midnight, our bodies ready for rest, then have turned our little world askew? We fell asleep in each other's arms, *mi corazón,* as we always do, secure and warm in the house you crafted for us, and our boy slept in the room next to us, ready for school the next day, dreaming whatever little boys dream, surrounded by toys you built for him, surrounded by the security he'd come to know and expect from you, from me. How could God have invaded our peace like that? I try not to remember.

When the flames consumed the cotton curtains by our bed, I thought we were lost. You screeched in pain, your hair a red halo about your face, your glowing hands pulling me to the floor on the other side of the bed. As we crawled to our boy's room and pulled him from the blankets, you howled your agony, my dear, dear Pablo, my love, my eternal love, my light. You howled as you dragged him and me to the ground outside, as you picked him up in your arms, as you pressed your red face near his little body, as you tried to breathe your essence into him.

Oh God oh God oh God oh God. How could this happen?

Memories swarm us sometimes and crowd our chest. Those who say time heals all wounds have not been wounded. Those who claim that memories fade with time have not stored memories. Memories are raw, always alive, as raw as when they first sprang to life. If it was a happy birth, the rawness can be relished, but the rawness of grief can only be pushed farther and farther into dark corners.

The Heavens Weep for Us

One can only pray that those corners can be kept dark, then darker, with time.

I remember the path of years, the years back to what we could call life, dear Pablo, what you and I could recapture and reinvent. For it's always about reinventing, filling the holes, staying away from the darkness, isn't it? The skin falling from you, the knives rebuilding you, your howls and screams bringing from our dark corners the rawness of the fire, the burn of loss. And in those years in the path, I recall the bravery in your withered arms, rebirthing legs, leather face. The re-emergence of your grin, the first time you laughed, the time your re-created hands held mine at the end of another torturous day. Happy memories trembled into the light. Burning ones receded into dusky spaces.

Today we were kids again. The afternoon sun was perfectly tilted, dappling through the treetops and throwing our wobbly shadows onto the asphalt as we rode rented bicycles at the resort. Your Bermuda shorts revealed your healing. I in my capris followed your lead as we wound our way through the manicured land of this beautiful place called Desert Breezes. Geraniums, heather, lilies, and bougainvillea blanketed the ground beneath palm trees of all varieties. The breeze, soothing indeed, rumpled your hair as you pedaled along awkwardly, glancing back at me to check on my progress as I wobbled along in your wake.

By the end of the hour, my dear Pablo, we were heady

with laughter. On an empty parking lot at one end of the resort, you challenged me to make better figure-eights than yours as you labored to maintain your balance on the bike. You teased me on my form, raced me to the opposite end of the parking lot, rode the rusty bicycle with your arms outstretched above your head, whooping and hollering and hoping no one would think mayhem was occurring and call the police. Your gray hair fluttered. The crinkles in the corners of your eyes held tears of utter abandon.

As I looked at your scars and the wrinkles in your legs, my dear, dear Pablo, I etched this scene into my core: a man in the twilight of his life, with his silver-haired wife, cavorting on bicycles, two people who have shared heaven and hell, who lost their angel, who take a simple day and infuse it with simple joy, simple love, and the purity of their desire to remember.

Other Stories by Thelma T. Reyna

"The Grapevine"

- *El Grito: A Journal of Contemporary Mexican-American Thought.* (Spring 1972). Octavio I. Romano-V (Ed.). Berkeley, CA: Quinto Sol Publications.
- *New Voices I: In Literature, Language, and Composition.* (1978). Jay Cline, Dan Donlan, James Flood, Coleen Goodwin, Russell Hill, Robert Probst, et al. (Eds.) Lexington, MA: Ginn & Company.

"Limousine"

- *Grito del Sol: A Chicano Quarterly.* (October-December 1976). Octavio I. Romano-V. (Ed.). Berkeley, CA: Tonatiuh International.
- *The Grito del Sol Collection.* (Winter 1984). Octavio I. Romano-V. (Ed.). Berkeley, CA: TQS Publications.

"A Bar of Soap"

- *Grito del Sol: A Chicano Quarterly.* (July-September 1977). Octavior I. Romano-V. (Ed.). Berkeley, CA: Tonatiuh International.
- *The Grito del Sol Collection.* (Winter 1984). Octavio I. Romano-V. (Ed.). Berkeley, CA: TQS Publications.

"Una Edad Muy Tierna, M'ija ("A Very Tender Age, My Daughter")

- *Grito del Sol: A Chicano Quarterly.* (July-September 1977). Octavior I. Romano-V. (Ed.). Berkeley, CA: Tonatiuh International.
- *The Grito del Sol Collection.* (Winter 1984). Octavio I. Romano-V. (Ed.). Berkeley, CA: TQS Publications.
- *Growing Up Chicana/o.* (1993). Tiffany Ana Lopez (Ed.). New York: Avon Books.

"Juan Romo"

- *New Voices II: In Literature, Language, and Composition.* (1978). Jay Cline, Dan Donlan, James Flood, Coleen Goodwin, Russell Hill, Robert Probst, et al. (Eds.) Lexington, MA: Ginn & Company.

LaVergne, TN USA
13 September 2009
157701LV00002B/3/P